Craig knew he'd made the right decision

The place smelled like cookies and pine. The song "I'll Be Home for Christmas" came to mind and it took him a second or two to realize that it was playing softly throughout the rooms downstairs.

There was a voice singing it, too, but from a distance. Singing live. With a tone so pure, so solid it gave him chills. Whoever that woman was, she should be in L.A., or on the stage, making millions on recordings.

"Oh! Sorry! I didn't hear the bell."

Craig wasn't sure which he noticed first—that the singing had stopped, or that he was now hearing the speaking rendition of that angelic voice.

"I'm looking for Marybeth Lawson." He stated his business, trying without success to break gazes with the violet-eyed blonde standing there with a plate of delicious-looking cookies in her hand.

The cook? His first thought.

And his second—what a waste.

"I'm Marybeth."

Two words. Innocuous. Everyday.

They changed his life.

Or they were going to.

Dear Reader,

Happy holidays! The season brings you two new Tara Taylor Quinn books—different from each other, but both straight from my heart. *At Close Range* comes from MIRA Books in December. But first up is *The Holiday Visitor,* which started out to be a fun romp. I should have known better. I don't "get" fun romp stories. I "get" emotionally intense, psychological looks at—everything. This time it's about love. Real love.

Now, here's where it's different. Marybeth Lawson has never had a boyfriend—and she has two heroes. James Winston Malone. And Craig McKellips. Craig was the one who gave me the most trouble. I was three-quarters of the way through the book, and I liked Craig okay. Problem was, I dreaded sitting down to write. I didn't have that feeling I get when I know a book is right. The bigger problem was that Craig didn't like himself. No matter how much I told him that I liked him just fine.

We had it out. I'd just finished a book, I had another one due and he was just going to have to get onto the page and out of my head. He lingered. And eventually I gave in. I always do. He apparently knew that about me.

A frantic week later, the book was done. And I loved Craig. More important, he loved himself. Now, don't get me wrong—the guy's not perfect. It's just that he had to be able to compete with James Malone. (I already loved him.)

So now you have it. A book with one heroine and two heroes. Happy reading!

Tara Taylor Quinn

P.S. I love to hear opinions! Write to me at staff@tarataylorquinn.com.

TARA TAYLOR QUINN
The Holiday Visitor

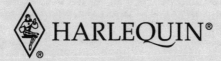

HARLEQUIN®

TORONTO • NEW YORK • LONDON
AMSTERDAM • PARIS • SYDNEY • HAMBURG
STOCKHOLM • ATHENS • TOKYO • MILAN • MADRID
PRAGUE • WARSAW • BUDAPEST • AUCKLAND

ISBN-13: 978-0-373-71527-5
ISBN-10:   0-373-71527-7

THE HOLIDAY VISITOR

This edition published by arrangement with Harlequin Books S.A.

® and TM are trademarks of the publisher. Trademarks indicated with ® are registered in the United States Patent and Trademark Office, the Canadian Trade Marks Office and in other countries.

www.eHarlequin.com

Printed in U.S.A.

ABOUT THE AUTHOR

With more than forty-five original novels, published in more than twenty languages, Tara Taylor Quinn is a *USA TODAY* bestselling author with over six million copies sold. She is known for delivering deeply emotional and psychologically astute novels. Ms. Quinn is a three-time finalist for the RWA RITA® Award, a multiple finalist for the National Reader's Choice Award, the Reviewer's Choice Award, the Booksellers' Best Award and the Holt Medallion, and appears regularly on the Waldenbooks bestseller list. Ms. Quinn recently married her college sweetheart and the couple currently lives in Ohio with their two very demanding and spoiled bosses: four-pound Taylor Marie and fifteen-pound rescue mutt/cockapoo, Jerry. When she's not writing Harlequin and MIRA books or fulfilling speaking engagements, Ms. Quinn loves to travel with her husband, stopping wherever the spirit takes them. They've been spotted in casinos and quaint little small-town antique shops all across the country.

Books by Tara Taylor Quinn

HARLEQUIN SUPERROMANCE

1225–WHAT DADDY DOESN'T KNOW
1272–SOMEBODY'S BABY*
1297–25 YEARS
   "Best Friends"
1309–THE PROMISE OF CHRISTMAS
1350–A CHILD'S WISH
1381–MERRY CHRISTMAS, BABIES
1428–SARA'S SON
1446–THE BABY GAMBLE†
1465–THE VALENTINE GIFT
   "Valentine's Daughters"
1500–TRUSTING RYAN

HARLEQUIN EVERLASTING LOVE

THE NIGHT WE MET

HARLEQUIN SINGLE TITLE

SHELTERED IN HIS ARMS*

*Shelter Valley stories
†Texas Hold 'Em

MIRA BOOKS

WHERE THE ROAD ENDS
STREET SMART
HIDDEN
IN PLAIN SIGHT
BEHIND CLOSED DOORS

For Chelsea Barney—
a beautiful young woman who is a new addition to
my family and who is very, very welcome here.

CHAPTER ONE

Friday, September 4, 1992

Dear James Winston Malone,
    They gave me your name as someone who wanted to write to someone else who had a parent that was a rape victim. My name is Marybeth Lawson. I am twelve years old. My mother was raped and killed last March. I just started eighth grade this year. If you want, we can write.
    Sincerely,
Marybeth Lawson

Tuesday, September 8, 1992

Dear Marybeth Lawson,
    I just turned thirteen last week. When will you be thirteen? I am in eighth grade, too. Writing's cool if that's what you want.
    Later,
James Malone

Saturday, September 12, 1992

Dear James,
    I only want to write if you do. But if you do, I do, too.

Sincerely,
Marybeth Lawson
P.S. I turn thirteen in January. I'm the youngest in my class because I started kindergarten early.

Tuesday, September 15, 1992

Dear Marybeth,

Okay, yeah, I want to. What classes are you taking? I have shop. I like it. I make things out of metal. Right now I'm working on a shelf for the bathroom wall for my mom's birthday. There's no medicine cabinet in there. We just moved and the place isn't all that great. I have art, too, and that's cool. English and the rest of that stuff I'm not so good at. I get okay grades, I just don't like 'em. Like who's ever going to need to know that that Shakespeare dude wrote about some guy who killed a king to be king and then had his wife commit suicide and then was beheaded? What kind of crap is that?

Sorry. You probably like that stuff.

Later,
James

Friday, September 18, 1992

Dear James,

I can't believe you're reading Shakespeare, too! In our school it's only the advanced classes who get it in eighth grade. I didn't much like *Macbeth,* either, but I loved *Romeo and Juliet.* They were almost our age. Not that that means anything. I wouldn't be in love if they paid me a million dollars. I just liked that they were such good friends that they would die for each other.

Someday I want to have a friend like that. (I can tell you that because you're just a piece of paper in another city and I'll never have to meet you or anything. That's what they said in counseling.) You're in counseling, too, right? So your mom lived? You're very lucky.

Write back soon,
Marybeth Lawson

Thursday, September 24, 1992

Marybeth,

Yeah, I'm in counseling just like you, but I don't like it much. And yes, my mom is alive. It's just me and her. I have to watch out for her, 'cause I'm all she's got. But, in case you're wondering, I'm pretty good at watching out so if you ever need to say something, go ahead. I won't make nothing of it. I could kinda be your good friend from far away, if you want. If you think that's corny then just forget I said it. I'm sorry your mom died.

Write back if you want,
James

Saturday, September 26, 1992.

Dear James,

I just got your letter. It's been over a week and I thought you weren't going to write back. I don't think what you said is corny at all. Why don't you like counseling? I think it's okay, it just doesn't seem to change anything. They say talking makes it better, but it doesn't. I don't want to talk about it. I just want to forget it. My dad quit already. He didn't like it, either. But he won't let me quit, yet. He's a great guy. I love him a lot. He can't help that he's so quiet and sad all the time now. I'm all he's got, too, and I try my best to take care of him. I've learned to cook some stuff pretty good, and I already knew how to clean. I ruined some of his white shirts in the wash but he didn't yell or anything. He just told me not to cry and went out and got more. He was always good that way. In the olden days he would've given me a hug, but we don't do that around here anymore. Does your mom? Sorry, you don't have to answer that if you don't want to.

School's okay. I was in cheerleading last year but dropped out this year. I'm doing gymnastics, though. I got my back handspring. I used to be too chicken, but I'm not anymore. My coach says that I could probably compete in high school if I want to. I don't know if I want to. My dad wouldn't have the time to come see meets anyway.

I like English. And math. Home ec is dumb. I already do all that stuff. But it's a required class to pass eighth grade so my dad said to just try to find something to like about it. I tried, but so far, nothing.

My dad's a manager of a company that makes computer parts. He golfs a lot. What does your mom do?

Write back soon,

Marybeth

Tuesday, September 29, 1992

Marybeth,

I came home from school today all bummed out 'cause I didn't make the baseball team and it was cool to have your letter here. I didn't really want to play baseball anyway. I like basketball better. I played that in my old school. But we just moved here to Colorado and I missed basketball tryouts. My mom says maybe next year. Your address says Santa Barbara, California. I looked it up on a map and it looks like it's right on the ocean. That's cool. I'd like to live on the ocean. My mom said it's a little town, not all rough and stuff like Los Angeles is on TV. I hope so and that you can be safe there.

My mom's a teacher. This year she has third grade. It's pretty cool. She likes kids and they seem to dig her pretty much, for a teacher and all.

Well, gotta go. Keep writing.

James Malone

P.S. Yeah, my mom hugs a lot—kinda too much but I don't really mind. I'd only ever tell you that, though, 'cause anyone else'd think I was a sissy or something. Sorry 'bout your dad.

P.S.S. If you want to talk about what happened to your mom, that's okay. Remember I'm just sorta a piece of paper.

Saturday, October 3, 1992

Dear James,

I'm sorry you didn't make the baseball team but I think baseball's boring. Guys just stand around while one or two throw and try to hit the ball and then there's a lot more standing around and stuff. Once in a while something exciting happens, like the time last month when that Brett guy from Kansas got his 3000th hit. They were playing my dad's team, the Angels, so I heard all the cheering. Anyway that kinda stuff only happens once in a while. My dad's really into sports. He watches them all the time now that Mom's gone. Mostly I hate them. Basketball's okay, though. It's fast.

No, I don't want to talk about my mom. I just want to forget. But it was nice of you to ask.

Santa Barbara's cool. I used to love it here. I wanted to move after what happened, but Dad couldn't because of his job and anyway, it wasn't like moving was going to make the memories go away. You got to, though, huh? That's cool. Sometimes I think life would be so much better if I were someplace where no one knew me or about what happened. I hate that kids at school sometimes look at me strange because they know. Like they feel sorry for me but no one talks to me. My dad says it's because they don't know what to say.

I used to have a best friend, Cara Williams, but she's hanging with some other kids now. I think I made her feel too weird 'cause I cried a lot in the beginning. I don't cry at all anymore. She still invites me to stuff, but I think it's 'cause her mother makes her. Anyway, she's still nice. I just don't want to be best friends anymore. I have to take care of my dad and do stuff here at home. And besides, all anyone ever tells me is, it's okay. It's going to be okay. And it's not, you know? It's not okay.

Sorry, I didn't mean to sound nasty or anything. I made sloppy joes for dinner tonight. My dad's golfing and there's no telling what time he'll be home and sloppy joes can sit on the stove till he gets here. My mom used to do stuff like that. Tonight I might babysit for the little girl next door. I do that sometimes while her parents play cards with their friends. They're home, but I'm fully in charge of Wendy. She's a year old and adorable. Plus they always have good snacks, like pizza rolls and I get paid. I'd do it even if I didn't, but I'm saving for a new bike.

Well, bye for now.

Marybeth Lawson

Wednesday, October 7, 1992

Marybeth Lawson,

Don't think I'm weird or anything and maybe I shouldn't say this, but I'm glad we're writing. I hope you are, too. My mom asked about you today when she saw that your letter came. She said to say hi. Don't worry, she doesn't see your letters and I don't tell her what we say. She's cool, though. She doesn't ask, except about how you are.

We went to court today. They changed our names. My mom and everyone said to do it. It's kind of like you said, people won't always be knowing about the past this way and we can live our lives here with all the new people who never knew us before. But they didn't know me by my name anyway, 'cause my mom wasn't married to my dad yet when she had me and so my name was different from theirs. I just don't think it's all that cool. I mean, it's like I have to pretend now. Like the old me was too rotten to live. Maybe, like Mom says, I'll understand when I'm older. I guess it's cool that she and I have the same last name now, instead of me having her maiden name. But anyway, if it's okay with you, I still want to be James Winston Malone here. That's who I really am and now you will be the only one who knows him. Unless that's too weird, then we don't have to.

See ya,
James Winston Malone

Saturday, October 10, 1992

Dear James Winston Malone,

Of course I'll call you James, still. It doesn't really

matter what we call each other, does it? I guess you'll get your letters if I address them that way. If you don't, I hope you write and tell me who to write to. But if you don't, you won't even get this anyway so, oh, well, anyway, tell your mom I said hi back.

Hey, I know what, why don't you call me something else, too? Then, with you, I can just be any old girl, 'cause unlike you, I'd kind of like to not have to be me anymore. I'm so sick of all those looks.

Anyway, how 'bout if you call me Candy? I'll be Candy Lawson. 'Kay?

My friend Cara likes a boy in the ninth grade. She saw him at the JV football game last night. I think she's dumb. I don't want to start liking boys for a really long time.

Well, I gotta go. My dad's golfing and I'm going with the people next door, the Mathers, they're Wendy's parents, you know the little girl I babysit, anyway I'm going with them to see *Batman Returns*. It's at the dollar theater. Have you seen it? Cara saw it this summer and said it's really cool.

Write back soon, 'kay?

Candy Lawson

CHAPTER TWO

Saturday, December 16, 2006

Dear Candy,

It's going to be a hard Christmas for both of us. Would that I could send a hug through a letter, my sweet friend, for you would surely have one now and anytime you opened an envelope from me.

Hard to believe that our parents both passed in the same year. And so young. I guess it's true that someone can die of a broken heart. I watched Mom slowly dwindle over the years, losing whatever zest she'd once had for life. It seemed as though she had the energy to see me raised, but once I left for college, she had no reason left to live.

Much like you say it was for your father.

In answer to your question, no, I won't be alone for Christmas. I was very glad to hear that you wouldn't be, as well. I picture you surrounded by people you care about.

I agree with what you said about heart—that it is the only true source that we can trust to guide us through life.

At the same time, the whole heart thing has me perplexed. If it's damaged by life's trials and tribulations, how much can we trust it? How much does it control us and how much can we control it?

Will I ever be able to open up and fully feel my heart, fully give it, or did the "incident" irrevocably change my ability to experience love on the deepest levels? Will I always be as I am now, moving through life without ever being fully engaged? Is there something I'm doing that keeps me trapped? Am I sabotaging myself? Or is this just the inevitable result to what happened when we were kids and a way of life for me that I can do nothing about—much like if I'd been in a skiing accident and lost a leg.

Tough questions. I look forward to your thoughts on this one.

In the meantime, know that I will be thinking about you through the season.

Yours,

James

"MARYBETH?"

Stuffing the letter she was reading into the writing desk drawer, Marybeth turned, smiling as a spry, little woman came through the kitchen into her living area, petting Brutus, two hundred and ten pounds of flesh and fur lounging in the doorway, as she passed.

"Hey! I didn't expect you until later." Jumping up, Marybeth stepped over the two-year-old mastiff and hugged Bonnie Mather, her surrogate mother from the time she was twelve.

"My garden club luncheon finished earlier than I thought—the speaker canceled."

"Well, come on in. The cookies are cooling, but I should be able to frost them if you want to wait." She'd told Bonnie she'd bake six dozen cookies to take to the soup kitchen.

"How about if I help?" Bonnie said, dropping the colorful cloth purse that was almost as big as she was onto Marybeth's sofa. "I might not make frosting as good as you do, but I can wield a mean knife."

"Yeah, right." Marybeth laughed. "My recipe is yours and you know it."

"That doesn't mean I can make it as well as you do." Bonnie stepped over Marybeth's dirt-colored pal on her way back out of the room. "I know you argued about having that dog, but knowing he's here with you sure gave your father peace of mind."

"I've gotten used to having him around."

"Your dad was beside himself when you first announced that you were going to run this place yourself."

That was putting it mildly. He'd done everything he could to get Marybeth to sell the bed-and-breakfast she'd inherited from a great-aunt she'd barely known.

"He didn't miss a single check-in from the time I opened until the day he died."

"Checking out the guests," Bonnie said.

Bonnie and Marybeth moved effortlessly in the professional kitchen of the Orange Blossom, assisting each other without word. As well they should considering the more than fourteen years they'd been cooking together. Bonnie had taught Marybeth, who had been written up in national travel magazines for her culinary talents and original recipes, most of what she knew.

Reaching around Marybeth for a stack of cooled bell-shaped cookies, Bonnie's arm rested along her waist. "How are you doing?" she asked softly.

"Okay," Marybeth said, whipping green food coloring into a bowl of confectioner's sugar and water icing. "Keeping busy. I have guests arriving today who'll be staying through next weekend. And then another check-in on the twenty-third staying until the thirty-first."

"Over Christmas?"

"Yeah."

"A family? Are they taking all four rooms?"

"No, just one person. In Juliet's room." Her lone holiday visitor, on a holiday that was going to be very lonely.

"You're coming over for the day, though, right?" Since her mother's death, Marybeth and her dad had spent every Christmas with Bonnie, Bob and Wendy Mather.

"I don't think so." Marybeth delivered what she knew wasn't going to be welcome news. She glanced at Bonnie, hoping the older woman would understand and not be hurt. "I…it's going to be hard this year and I think it'd be better if I had a change. I feel like I need to do something different, to, I don't know, start my own life or something." It made a whole lot more sense when she thought about it to herself, than it did when she said it out loud. "Besides," she added, "I don't want to be a downer on your holiday."

"We loved your dad, too, missy," Bonnie said in her most motherly voice. "We'll all be missing him. Please come."

"I…maybe," Marybeth told her, really feeling like she wouldn't. Couldn't. Not this first Christmas anyway. "I have to see what my guest is going to be doing."

"You're only responsible for breakfast and evening libations," Bonnie said. "You'll have the rest of the day free."

"I was thinking about going to the beach. Or…I don't know. Can I let you know?"

"Of course. And if you say no and change your mind, you can drop in, too. You know that. You don't need an invitation."

Meeting Bonnie's gaze, Marybeth blinked back the tears she was so valiantly trying to prevent. "Thank you."

"It'll be strange having Christmas without you."

"I know. I just…I have to do this. Okay?"

Bonnie's okay didn't sound happy. Or even satisfied. But at least the dreaded chore of telling her was done.

"So what was that you were reading when I came in?" Bonnie asked after a few minutes of silence as the two of them, spreaders in hand, covered dozens of sugar cookie renditions of Santas and bells and Christmas trees with red and green and white frosting and sprinkles.

Marybeth grabbed the nonpareils. They'd always been her favorites—even way back when her mom had been the one doing the baking. "A letter from James."

"A recent one?"

"Yeah. His mom died this year, too."

"So you're still writing to him."

"Mmm-hmm."

"Fourteen years and he continues to write regularly?"

"Yes."

"I didn't realize you were still in touch with him."

"Of course I am." She was addicted to him. With every single one of the hundreds of letters she'd received from James over the years, she'd read and reread the most recent until she heard from him again. And if something in her life was particularly challenging, if she needed some extra strength, she'd pull out the plastic storage boxes under her bed and reread some of the others, as well. "Why wouldn't I be?" she asked the person she was closest to in the world next to James.

"I don't know." Bonnie's shrug, the way she was concentrating so hard on putting little Christmas tree sugar shapes in a row along the cookie to make them look like a string of lights, caught Marybeth's attention. "It's just that I worry about you."

"About me?" No way. Those days were long gone. She didn't need sympathy anymore. Or worry. She was a big girl now. All grown up, in control and happy with her life. "And James?"

"Not you and James. I wish there was a you and James."
Bonnie's reply wasn't timid. "Look at you, sweetie. You're
twenty-six years old and gorgeous with those blue eyes and
blond hair, and you haven't so much as had a date that I know
of since you graduated from college three years ago and took
over this place."

"That has nothing to do with James."

"Doesn't it?"

"Of course not." Frost, sprinkle, lay out to dry. Frost, sprinkle,
lay out to dry. She worked her way through a pile of stars.

"Then what does it have to do with? Your mother?"

"No!" Her mother's death had been fourteen years ago.
She'd lived before then. And since. So why did people
continue to seem to tie every single thing in her life back to
that one event? "It's not that I have a problem with dating,"
she said. "I'm not afraid. I have no aversions. I simply haven't
yet met a man who inspires any feeling in me. There's no attraction. No spark."

"What about with James?"

"I've never even seen a picture of him, how could there be
an attraction?"

"What about feelings of affection?"

"Of course I have feelings for James. How could I not?
He's my best friend. I can tell him anything."

"This guy you've never met."

"Right."

"You sure you aren't using him as an excuse not to open
up too completely to any of the real, flesh-and-blood people
in your life?"

"I open up to you. You're flesh and blood."

"I'm different," Bonnie said. "I'm talking about people
out there in the world. Someone you could actually build a
life with."

Marybeth frosted. Cookies for Bonnie. Cookies for the senior center. Cookies for here. With any luck, she'd be done in time to have a tray of them on the desk at check-in by three o'clock for her visitors to enjoy.

"I have a life," she said after taking time to think about what Bonnie had said. "James isn't taking the place of any other relationships," she continued. "He's his own relationship. We have these ongoing philosophical discussions that always hit home with me. Probably because, based on the unusual nature of our relationship, we talk about things that people don't usually share. You know, deep, random thoughts, illogical matters of the heart and head and life. Observations that generally pass through your mind and are forgotten in the business of daily living." She'd been discussing the meaning of life with James for fourteen years and wasn't about to stop now. Wasn't sure she could even if she wanted to.

"You have no idea how many times we help each other find solutions to challenges we're facing. We don't judge each other. We just talk."

"All things you could be doing with a spouse."

"Do you and Bob do them?"

Bonnie's silence was answer enough.

"James is my peace, Bonnie. My solace and support. He's my kind inner voice counteracting my inner critic who, as you know, so often tries to rule my life. He's not a romance. Or a partner in life."

Marybeth finished the stars and the Santas and moved on to help Bonnie with the trees. And because her friend remained silent, she continued to talk. "James is like this ethereal being who, unlike any spiritual, omniscient being, knows nothing of my everyday life, you know? And he shares nothing of his. We share a past, a dark time. We both went through the same thing at the same time in our lives. That's it."

"I hope so, my dear," Bonnie said as they finished up. "I just know that your idea of normal isn't healthy. You, here all alone, living vicariously through the people who parade in and out of this inn."

"I take care of them. It's my job. My livelihood. And I like it."

"I know you do, sweetie, and I'm thrilled that you've found something that satisfies you. I just wish you had a private life, too."

She did have a private life. Not a single one of her guests had ever stepped foot beyond the public parts of the house. What went on out there was work. What went on back here was her life.

She simply hadn't found anyone she wanted to share that life with in the way Bonnie meant. Marybeth didn't really even want to try.

"I'm not lonely," she told her pseudomother. "But if I ever start to feel that way, I promise you, I'll find someone. I'll start frequenting the personal ads if I have to."

"You wouldn't have to," Bonnie assured her. "I know of a half dozen people in this town who'd love to take you out."

So did she. Unfortunately none of them interested her in the least.

CRAIG ANTHONY MCKELLIPS drove slowly by the Orange Blossom Bed-and-Breakfast, every one of his senses reeling with sensation. His mouth watered. He could practically taste the oranges that were pungently ready for picking on the trees that lined both sides of the lot, separating the freshly painted white Victorian home—complete with grand balconies upstairs and an even grander porch down—from the pictur-esque old homes on either side.

Sweating in spite of the crisp fifty-nine-degree temperature, Craig pushed the button to lower his window a bit and was hit with the sweet scents wafting from the wildly colorful, but perfectly tended flower gardens in manicured rings in the yard and lining the entire front of the house. He could taste a hint of salt in the air, letting him know that he was by the ocean again. By nightfall he'd be feeling the salty residue on his skin.

And the quiet. It amazed him! This California coastal town, maybe an hour's drive from the Los Angeles he'd known as a kid, was the exact antithesis of the noisy, frenetic southern California he'd grown up in.

A perfect place to spend his first Christmas alone—his first Christmas since his mother passed away.

Satisfying himself that he knew where the house was, Craig drove by for now. Judging by the empty, five-car parking lot down a small hill to the side of the house, none of the other guests had arrived—or else were out for the day. Check-in wasn't until three.

Would the other guests be there at three, too? Filling the house with chaos and confusion, noise, distracting their hostess? Would he know who she was? She might not look like the photo he'd seen of her in the travel brochure. Maybe she had an employee who handled registration.

Driving slowly through the small town, Craig used the breathing techniques he'd perfected over the years to quiet his mind. After months of constant push to get through all of the commissions that were due by Christmas, he needed this break from the studio that consumed so much of his life.

And from the constant drive to create.

He also needed the inner calm his work brought.

When he couldn't settle the energy thrumming through him, Craig found a spot close to the water and parked. He thought about calling Jenny. His wife should just about be landing in Paris.

But he didn't.

Reaching over, he locked his cell phone in the glove box of the rental car.

What he needed was a good long walk on the beach.

"MERRY CHRISTMAS, everyone!" Marybeth turned to wave at the gathering of wheelchairs in the recreation room of the seniors' center the Saturday before Christmas, bearing the collective weights of people who'd grown dear to her over the three years she'd been catering their Christmas lunch party. This year she'd brought homemade ornaments for them to hang on their bedposts—ornaments she'd crocheted during the evenings while she and Brutus watched television.

She lingered, helping lay out all the food, handing out the gifts and chatting with everyone. They pressed her to join them for the meal, but she bowed out claiming her arriving guest as her excuse.

Leaving the seniors' center she headed over to the Mathers's to unload the pile of gifts she had for them on the backseat of her Expedition. Though Bonnie had tried all week to get her to change her mind, Marybeth still thought she wanted to be alone this first Christmas without her dad.

"I can't believe you aren't coming over on Monday," fifteen-year-old Wendy said as she helped Marybeth carry in packages.

Her dad was still at work and her mother was at the soup kitchen.

"It's just this one year," Marybeth told the teenager who was as much daughter and sister to her as longtime neighbor. "I think it'll be easier if I'm not following the same traditions, you know?"

"I get it," Wendy said. "I'm not sure Mom does, but she'll come around. She always does."

"Hey," Marybeth said, nudging the younger girl. "How'd your date go last night?"

"With Randy?" Wendy had had a crush on the boy from their church for months and he'd finally asked her out.

"Who else?"

Wendy's blush was answer enough. "It was good," she said and Marybeth knew immediately that this was one of those times when the word was a definite understatement.

Finished with the presents, Wendy walked with Marybeth back to her car. "Who was your first boyfriend? I don't remember him."

"That's because I never really had one," she said. "And it's a good thing because you'd have been bugging us all the time if I had."

"No," Wendy said, frowning. "Seriously. What about that first time you met someone and just knew you'd die if he didn't like you as much as you liked him?"

Warning bells ringing, Marybeth stopped by the door of her car. "I never met anyone who made me feel that way," she said slowly, while her mind raced ahead. "But I knew some girls who did," she added, remembering how frantic her friend Cara had been their last year in junior high. The girl had even run away from home to be with the guy she'd thought was her soul mate. "And what I can tell you is that as intense as those feelings are, they can't be trusted until you're a bit older. Right now, they aren't just from the heart, but get confused and mixed up with hormonal changes, too."

Bonnie, don't hate me. I hope I'm not screwing this up.

"I don't know," Wendy said. "I mean, even hearing Randy's laugh makes me all warm inside."

No. Not this soon. Please. "Have you talked to your mom about this?"

"Sorta. She likes Randy. She likes his parents, too. She just tells me to be careful, but that's not the point. I am careful. I'm a good girl. How could I not be with you and Mom in my life?"

Marybeth grinned with the girl.

"I'm not going to do anything crazy," Wendy said, growing serious. "I'm just *going* crazy with these feelings. I'll die if he doesn't ask me out again."

"No, you won't." Marybeth gave the girl a hug. "You'll call me and come over for the weekend and we'll eat tacos and ice cream and watch movies that make us cry and talk bad about Randy and you'll find someone else to like before you know it."

"You didn't."

"I didn't find a Randy, either." Marybeth thanked fate for the little help finding a comeback on that one. "Not all women are meant to fall in love. If you are, then it'll happen. And if not, no amount of wishing or pushing can make it happen. Wishing and pushing will only make you make mistakes. And bring unhappiness."

"I don't get it," Wendy said as Marybeth climbed into her SUV.

"Get what?"

"You. I mean, look at you. You've got it all. Looks, brains, money. You're skinny and gorgeous. Any guy would be a fool not to fall for you."

"But in order for it to work, I'd have to fall for him, too," Marybeth said, wondering if it was her father's death, leaving her all alone in the world, that was bringing out this sudden urge in the Mathers for her to find a mate. "I'm not opposed to falling in love, sweetie," she told her friend. "I just haven't. And I'm okay with that. Most days, I think I prefer it that way."

"I sure wouldn't," Wendy said with a chuckle. "Think about Christmas," she called out as Marybeth drove off.

She agreed that she would. But she didn't think she was going to change her mind.

HE'D STEPPED into a Christmas wonderland. He should have suspected when he'd noticed that the garden stakes interspersed throughout the flowers were of old world Santa and snowman design, and seen the lights hiding in the garland bordering the porch railing. Red bows dotted the garland and the pine smell teased his nostrils with memories of long ago Christmases with his parents at their cabin in Northern California.

The outside of the Orange Blossom Inn was festive. Still, it did nothing to prepare Craig for the spectacular sight as he stepped inside. From the felt and sequined door hangings and stops, to the intricately stitched wall hangings, from the colorful stockings hanging from every door handle, to the various collections of figurines sitting on every available surface, Craig's gaze moved around the foyer and reception area and beyond to the enormous, heavily decorated Christmas tree adorning the formal parlor to his right. Brightly lit, with the colored lights he preferred over the small white lights that had become so popular, the tree promised hours of sightseeing. It looked like every single ornament on the edifice was homemade.

No porcelain or glass or anything else that appeared the least bit factory influenced. Oddly out of place, considering the rest of Christmas abundance around him, was the bare wood floor beneath and around the tree.

Where were the gaily wrapped and decorated packages the tableau cried out for?

An electric train, much like the collector's one he and his father had worked on when he'd been a kid—complete with the lighted town buildings and trees and people—filled a table that took up an entire wall of the parlor. It chugged softly along, the only moving entity in the room.

The place smelled like cookies and pine and with a long, deep breath, Craig knew he'd made the right decision. The song "I'll Be Home For Christmas" came to mind and it took him a second or two to realize that it was playing softly.

There was a voice singing it, too, but from a distance. Singing live. With a tone so pure, so solid it gave him chills. Whoever that woman was, she should be in L.A., or on the stage, making millions on recordings.

"Oh! Sorry! I didn't hear the bell."

Craig wasn't sure which he noticed first, that the singing had stopped, or that the owner of that voice he was hearing was speaking another rendition of that angelic gift.

"I'm looking for Marybeth Lawson," he stated his business, trying, without success, to break gazes with the violet-eyed blonde standing there holding a plate of delicious-looking cookies.

The cook? Was his first thought.

And his second—what a waste.

"I'm Marybeth."

Two words. Innocuous. Everyday.

They changed his life.

Or they were going to.

Craig couldn't explain the impression. Nor could he argue with it. It simply was. With or without his cooperation or acceptance.

CHAPTER THREE

CRAIG MCKELLIPS was much younger than the doddering, elderly gentleman who opted to spend Christmas alone guest she'd expected. And gorgeous. Tall, with dark golden, slightly long hair he was the epitome of every bronze god Marybeth had ever imagined. Skin, eyes, expression—everywhere she looked the man glowed.

Not that she was looking, Marybeth assured herself a couple of hours after Craig had checked in. The man was her guest. One of the hundreds she'd hosted in the three years since she'd opened the Orange Blossom for business. He was back downstairs, seemingly completely satisfied with Juliet's room, ready for the evening cocktail she advertised in her brochure and on the Internet.

The only reason she was noticing him so intensely was because of her recent conversation with Wendy. She'd been thinking about the feelings the girl had described for Randy that afternoon.

Trying to imagine how infatuation felt so that she knew how to advise the girl. How to help the teenager keep herself away from temptation and out of trouble.

Craig McKellips stood in the doorway to the parlor, still looking godlike in spite of—or because of?—having freshened up, his eyes trained on the far side of the room and the lump lying in the archway leading to the kitchen and the private part of the house.

"I'm assuming that's yours?" he asked, staring, hands resting on either side of the open French doors.

"Yeah." She tried to smile reassuringly, as she did every evening that she introduced her family member to their guests, but couldn't seem to pull it off. Neither could she walk up to him, shake his hand as he joined her. She was nervous.

And there was absolutely no reason why she should be. She'd hosted many single men over the years.

"His name's Brutus." She was supposed to be telling him that the oversize dog was friendly. A sweetheart. She meant to. But stood there feeling like an adolescent with a crush instead.

Or, at least, reminding herself of how Cara had acted in eighth grade. How Wendy had sounded that afternoon.

Nodding, Craig stood still, keeping his distance from Brutus, though to give him credit, he looked more respectful than leery.

"Having him here is a good idea," he said. "With your home open to the public, strangers coming and going, you're wise to take precautions."

Very perceptive. Not that any of the guests ever knew that Marybeth stayed in the back part of the house alone. As she'd told Bonnie last week, up until her father's death two months ago, he'd been there to meet every guest she had. Had insisted she send him her guest register at the beginning of every week.

It had been the only time she'd ever seen him.

"He doesn't bite unless I give the command." Her suddenly lame brain was spitting out all the wrong things.

Dropping his arms, Craig advanced slowly, then knelt, his long, gorgeous legs bending beneath him as he called Brutus over. The two-hundred-plus-pound lug took half a minute to drag himself to a standing position and saunter over. Sitting a head above their only guest, Brutus stared the man down.

"Good boy," Craig said, holding out a hand and Marybeth

nearly dropped the glass she'd been holding. Not once in three years had a guest touched Brutus without her right there holding the dog and guiding the introductions.

Brutus, kind being that he was, didn't rebuke Craig for his insolence. Instead he sniffed the hand beneath his nose and then sat, with only a small frown on his face, and accepted the petting that was, after all, his due.

"White wine or red?" Marybeth asked, turning to the cherrywood bar against one wall.

"White, please." Even his voice warmed the space around him.

And suddenly, Marybeth heard Wendy's voice in her head, "even his laugh makes me feel warm."

What in the hell was going on here?

"Frosty the Snowman" played in the background—an old Partridge Family rendition that sounded more like a love ballad than a friendly rollick—leaving Marybeth embarrassed, though she had no idea why.

She didn't meet his gaze as she handed him the wine. But she almost dropped the glass when his knuckles brushed against hers.

"There's, uh, cheese and crackers and, um, fresh fruit on the bar. Help yourself," she invited, having to concentrate to remember what food she'd just carried out.

She then went to turn down the temperature on the thermostat.

"Aren't you joining me?" He gestured to the wine. "It's impolite to drink alone."

"Not when you're the only guest it isn't." She couldn't drink with him. He was a guest.

Though the relaxation she might find with a glass of wine sounded heavenly at the moment. She had too much Wendy and teenage love on the brain.

"Well, it's not healthy," he said, still holding the completely full glass. "Once you start drinking alone, it gets easier and easier and, before you know it, you're pouring yourself a glass in the middle of the afternoon."

Frowning, Marybeth wondered if she should have served any alcohol at all. If he had a problem...

It wasn't her problem. He was a grown man. An adult—albeit a much younger one than she'd assumed. He couldn't be much more than twenty-six or seven. Her age...

"You sound as though you're speaking from experience."

"Not my own," he told her. "I used to...know...someone...."

Ah. Someone close to him if she had to guess. Not that it mattered to her.

"Yes, well, in that case, I'll have one small glass."

What? She didn't want any wine. Not really. She was a hostess. Working.

And while she was pouring the drink she didn't want, Marybeth wasted brain cells wondering what her guest thought of her red, heavily embroidered, beaded and appliquéd Christmas sweater, rather than if he liked the food she'd presented.

"You're spilling."

Oh, God. She was. Over her fingers. Setting down the bottle, Marybeth tried to come up with a pithy, logical and sensible excuse for overfilling her glass. To no avail.

But cleaning it up gave her a minute to berate herself. Collect herself. Cool down.

Was she attracted to this man?

Was this...this energy running through her body what Wendy had been talking about?

"So..." she asked, dropping the soaked napkins in the metal bin—it, too, matched the seasonal decor—beside the bar. "Who brings you to Santa Barbara for the holiday?" Busywork done, she faced him.

Craig choked midsip. *"Who?"*

"Can I get you some water?"

"No." Another slight cough. "I'm fine. What did you mean, who?" Even though he was still emitting half coughs, his gaze was piercing. Too piercing.

"Well…" Marybeth led the way over to a conversational grouping of antique sofas in front of the gas fireplace, burning merrily for the occasion. To go with the air-conditioning she'd also just switched on. "It's Christmas," she said, sitting farthest from the tree while Brutus reclaimed his spot guarding their quarters. "I can't imagine you're here on business. Or for a beach holiday on Christmas Day. I assumed whoever you're spending the holiday with didn't have enough beds to accommodate everyone…."

"I'm spending the holiday with myself."

He was available. Marybeth glanced at the third finger of his left hand. No wedding band.

No rings on those hands period.

"What about your parents?" The question came without her usual forethought and Marybeth wondered if she should escape to her private quarters, lock herself up or something until the craziness that was consuming her passed.

Grace, the woman who came in to help Marybeth clean, had had a cold a week or two ago. Perhaps she'd contracted some latent germ from the woman and the microscopic mite had suddenly decided to spring to life in her groin area.

"I'm sorry," she added when he hesitated. "I don't know what's gotten into me." She stood. "I don't mean to pry. I'll just leave you to your evening. Remember, if you leave after seven, to take your key with you. The doors lock automatically—"

All information she'd already given him.

"No!" Craig stood, as well, his jeans and sweater a perfect fit on his tall, athletic body. She loved how his hair curled up over his collar. "Please, don't go," he was saying while she ogled him. "Unless you have something else to do, that is. I'd…love the company."

She had to make breakfast. Sometime before six in the morning. And finish gluing together the clay pot snowman ornaments she was making for the refreshment tables at tomorrow night's Christmas Eve services.

"I mean, I've never stayed at one of these before," he said, sounding not the least bit awkward. "If it's not proper, or something, for you to visit with your guests, I understand, I just thought…well, it is the holidays and I'm sure you have a million things to do—family that's waiting for you."

That was her opening. Or closing, she meant. Her escape.

"No, actually, I generally mingle during happy hour," she heard herself admit the very thing she'd decided not to mention. "In case anyone has questions about the area, or needs directions or suggestions for dinner. Speaking of which, there's a binder here filled with all of the places to eat in town." She grabbed the familiar, well-used book and handed it to him. "I've made notes on the ones I think are exceptional. And discarded a couple that I no longer feel comfortable recommending. You're welcome to take a look. Only a few will be open on Christmas Day, so you might want to choose early. They're marked. I should make a reservation for you as soon as possible…"

No man should smell so good. It had to be a sin.

"Okay, I'll take a look," Craig said when she stopped to catch her breath. And let her brain catch up with her. "I hadn't really thought about Christmas dinner," he admitted, opening the black book. "I'll probably just spend the day on the beach. Or driving along the coast. I've always wanted to do that."

"The trip up State Route One is remarkable." There. A good answer. "If you've never taken it before, you might want to give it a try. It's slow going in some parts, but follows the coast. You can go all the way to San Francisco without losing sight of the ocean for more than a few minutes."

"San Francisco. That's, what, about three hours from here?"

"Three or four, depending on how fast you drive. And on traffic." No one liked to be rushed, or run out of time. Which would explain why she wanted to stand there with him for…a long time.

He nodded. And she realized that they'd been looking each other straight in the eye for too many seconds. She was going to look away. To take a sip of wine.

"My parents are both gone," he said, answering her earlier question.

Her heart filled with compassion. Empathy. "I'm so sorry. Recently?"

And as his golden-brown eyes glistened, continuing to speak to her even before he spoke again, Marybeth knew that this man was special. Different.

"My dad's been gone a long time," he said with little emotion. And then swallowed. "Mom died this past year. Kidney problems."

"Do you have brothers and sisters?" Maybe they were all at spouses' family homes for the holidays. Maybe they'd invited him and he, not wanting to crash the party, had declined. Maybe he had a sibling here, in Santa Barbara….

The thoughts chased themselves around her mind more quickly than she could keep up with them. She just knew she didn't want him to be alone. Didn't want him to have to know how alone felt.

"I'm an only child," he told her and Marybeth peered across the room. Sipped her wine. Studied the lights on the tree, the patterns in light color repetition. There weren't any patterns.

"Me, too." The words were soft, only half spoken, really.

She was breaking cardinal rule numbers one through ten. Marybeth did not speak about her private life to her guests. Ever. Or drink with them. Or open her heart to them. Or feel attraction…

"You're an only child?" The question was quiet, respectful. His head was cocked slightly as he watched her.

When her usual yes, without further elaboration, wasn't enough, Marybeth knew she was in trouble.

"My parents are both dead."

She was really reacting to this guy.

Was she just vicariously living Wendy's feelings for Randy? Suffering from transference?

Was it the holidays?

"Recently?"

She couldn't stop looking at him. "My mom died when I was a kid. An…accident. Dad passed just this year. He had a heart attack on the tennis court."

"Completely unexpected."

She nodded. "I…have a friend, who lost a parent this year, too." Thoughts of James while she was sitting here attracted to another man made the whole situation that much more surreal.

James should be sitting in her living room, making her tongue-tied and uneven. Not this stranger. She and James had history. Things that could never, ever be duplicated. They understood each other on levels most people didn't even know existed.

She needed him this week. More than ever.

And he'd refused to meet her. Ever.

"Someone here locally?"

He'd promised, from the ripe age of thirteen, that he'd always be there for her. "No," she said. "He's in Colorado." Or at least his mailing address was.

"With family?"

She had no idea how to answer that. The truth—that she

didn't know if James had any family other than the mother who'd just died, didn't even know if he was married, or living with a woman, or gay for that matter—would be too hard to explain in light of the fact that she'd just called him a friend.

And the greater truth—that her best friend since junior high school was a pen pal she'd never met—wasn't sharing material. Ever. With anyone.

"He's not alone," she said in the end. It was the only information pertinent to the current conversation.

"And what about you?" Craig's lids lowered slightly as he asked the question.

"I…" She parried personal questions. Always. And not just since she'd become the keeper of a house filled with others' memories in the making, either.

The silence was long enough for him to bow out of the conversation. To let her off the hook.

He didn't. He simply sat there. Watching her. Waiting.

Time to clean up the cheese and crackers. To call Brutus over. To start breakfast. Or glue something.

"Yes." Dammit. She'd known the word was coming. Should have tried harder to prevent it from slipping out. She had no idea where any of this could go.

No idea if he even noticed she was alive, other than as a hostess he was paying to take care of him for a few days.

"My surrogate family wants me to come over, as Dad and I have done every year since Mom died."

"But you turned them down?" He didn't sound critical. Or even as though he thought her crazy.

"I told them I was working. Breakfasts don't cook and linens don't get changed by themselves and I sure wasn't going to call my cleaning lady, Grace, away from her family."

Frowning, Craig set his glass on the claw-foot, cherry coffee table. "I'm keeping you away from your friends? I can go—"

"No!" What was it about him? And her? "I'd stay home whether you were here or not. Truly. I already told them I wasn't coming."

Her choice to live her life alone might seem odd to most people, but she didn't have to justify herself. Nor would she. She was all grown up now. An adult. Her life was her own.

And she was happy.

She was also completely turned on for the first time in her life.

CHAPTER FOUR

CRAIG TRIED TO CALL Jenny when he went back to his room to grab a jacket before heading out for the short walk to a quaint little diner he'd seen about a block away from the inn. When she didn't pick up, he stifled his frustration mixed with relief, quickly left a message letting her know that he'd arrived in Santa Barbara, that he was hoping she'd arrived safely, as well, and that he'd call her again in a day or so, reception allowing.

"Love you." His final words were offered with sincerity.

Her flight might have been delayed. Or she could be out. Or with her family and not able to answer. She could have left her cell phone in her room. Or failed to charge it. One thing was for certain. If Miss Jenny Fournier-Chevalier didn't end up safely at her folks' castle situated on richly grown acres of French countryside, Craig McKellips would be hearing about it.

HE DIDN'T SEE his hostess again that night. Though he made eating a business, tackling the task efficiently, rather than lingering and appreciating the anomaly of free time, the door to her quarters had been firmly closed when he returned to the Orange Blossom. The light shining from beneath her door had called to him, though.

He'd thought about knocking. And thought about Brutus and privacy and the fact that he had nothing to offer the young, vibrant woman who lived on the other side of that portal—no matter how much he wanted to be in her presence. He was married. More, he had secrets, things Marybeth Lawson couldn't ever know, things that prevented them from ever being more than casual acquaintances.

Craig spent more hours than he'd have liked in front of the window in the Juliet room that night, and again, the next morning staring at the ocean in the distance—unwinding, thinking, trying to come to terms with his life—until it was finally time to head downstairs to breakfast. Dressed in baggy black shorts and a white polo shirt topped with a black sweater to protect him from ocean breezes, he forced himself to take the steps one at a time when what he wanted to do was jog the whole way.

"Have you eaten?" he asked his beautiful hostess as he entered the dining room to see her filling a glass with orange juice from an antique-looking glass pitcher, at a table set for one.

She wore black jeans. A white cotton top that hugged her thin waist and outlined the swell of her breasts, and another one of those adorable Christmas sweaters—this one a cardigan sporting the embroidered design of dalmatians and hearths with stockings hanging from them.

"Good morning!" She seemed to be having just as hard a time not staring at him as he was not staring at her. "No, I haven't eaten," she continued, heading over to a heated sideboard that had to be portable because it looked identical to the one he'd seen in the living room the night before—scarred leg and all. "I wait until everyone else is finished and take whatever's left over."

"Since everyone else is just me, would it be completely awkward for you if I asked you to join me?" he asked without any remorse at all. "It being Christmas Eve and all, and I won't eat much if I think I'm taking food from your mouth and…"

Hands in his pockets, feeling plain good for a moment, he was prepared to go on and on.

"Okay!" With a grin, she smiled at him. "But only because it's a holiday and I'd hate to eat alone, too, if I were you."

While ordinarily Craig would more than bristle at being a target of pity—even in play—if it meant Marybeth was joining him, he'd accept as much pity as she wanted to hand out.

And then, minutes later, as she glanced at his hand, her smile faded.

"You're wearing a wedding ring this morning."

They were just starting the first course—a concoction of fresh fruit and yogurt and he didn't know what, served in parfait glasses. Or rather, he was. She sat, slightly slouched, frowning, her spoon poised above her dish, watching him.

He nodded. "This is great. Delicious. Did you make it yourself?"

"Yeah. I do all my own cooking. From scratch and I use freshly picked fruits and vegetables whenever possible." Her voice had no inflection at all.

She took a bite. Chewed, her gaze distant.

"I'm married."

There. That was done.

"I didn't notice the ring last night."

"I didn't have it on."

She didn't say anything. He felt like an A-class jerk.

"Jenny and I…we're…"

What was he doing? This woman was a stranger to him. Or should be.

"It's okay," she said, jumping up in spite of the fact that she'd only taken the one bite. "I don't mean to pry. I'll bring in the casserole. Do you prefer sausage, bacon or both?"

"Sausage, please."

And she was gone, leaving him brimming with frustration at his own inadequacies.

He was no less fretful when his beautiful hostess returned

less than two minutes later, two plates laden with an egg-and-sausage concoction, some kind of rosemary-looking potatoes and garnished with more fruit, in her hands.

"Jenny's older than I am." He gave her the most innocuous fact of his life. "By five years."

"Oh." She sat. Cut a piece of casserole. Put it in her mouth. Chewed. "Coffee?" She held up the pot.

Shaking his head, Craig watched her take another bite. Watched her lips.

And attacked his own breakfast.

"We're both artists," he offered, several minutes into the meal when all he could think about was touching his hostess' hands to see if they were as soft as they looked.

"Painters?"

He reached for the coffeepot. She got there first and filled his cup for him. A wifely thing to do.

"She paints. I sculpt. Sort of."

"What does that mean?" A small, impersonal smile curved her lips and Craig felt himself sinking again.

"I build things out of metal. Wall scenes. Pictures. Even furniture. Pretty much anything I'm commissioned to do." A simplistic explanation, but it would suffice. His art, his career, didn't matter here.

"Do you work under your own name?"

"Yes." Such a hazy distinction between duplicity and truth.

Trying to follow her lead, to get them back to the level of married guest with innkeeper, he answered all of her questions as they finished the main course, meeting some internal need he didn't understand as he told her about himself. He didn't own a retail shop, preferring to sell his stuff at shows, but he did have a studio on his property. No, he and his wife didn't share workspace. Her studio was the whole upstairs of the cabin they'd had built the year before. He used all kinds of metals in his work and had perfected a way to colorize in a technique similar to ceramics with special paints and repeated firings of the metal. And while he'd been all around the country, these days he had very little time to be out on the road hocking his wares due to the numbers of commissioned orders he was receiving.

"We have a fairly well-known art show not far from here," she said over her last bite of casserole. She licked her fork. He followed the path her tongue took. "It's sometime in June and draws artists from all over the States."

"I know." He had to look away as his body responded to the innocent stimuli. "I'm signed up for it. That's actually how I came to be here now. They sent an acceptance packet with local information. Your ad was one of the many offering accommodations."

Think work, man. Work and secrets. And Jenny.

"Do I have you booked then?" She didn't seem unhappy about that.

"Not yet." He'd needed to check things out first. Always. No matter what he did. "But I plan to do that before I leave."

He could do this. Have a friend. Jenny had many—both male and female. He'd tell her about Marybeth. Marybeth knew he was married. It was all okay. Whether he was married or not, he could never be more than passing-through friends with Marybeth Lawson, anyway. There were reasons for that, too.

"Good. Now's the time to do it." Marybeth cleared their plates, leaving them on the sideboard as she brought over the coffee cake that had been warming. "I've only been open three years, but all three summers were completely booked. Every single night from May until September."

"I hope you have people in here helping you."

"A woman comes in and cleans, but I pretty much do the rest myself. I like it that way."

"Seven days a week for three months straight? What about time off?"

"Other than cooking, I'm off a good part of each day unless I'm doing the cleaning. I'm here for breakfast, and for check-in at three. And for evening libations. Otherwise I come and go."

"But you don't have a full day off? Not even one?"

Putting a too big piece of mouthwatering cake on a plate in front of him, Marybeth shrugged. "What for?"

The response tugged at him.

HE ATE EVERY BITE of the huge piece of caramel walnut coffee cake she'd made last night after she'd heard Craig come in from dinner. It had been her father's favorite. A family tradition to have it on Christmas Eve. One of the few that Marybeth had kept up after her mother's death.

One of the few her father had acknowledged. She hadn't planned on making it this year. Then Craig McKellips had walked through the door and she'd been doing all sorts of crazy things.

Like sitting down to breakfast with a guest. Like feeling more hungry for the guest than for the food she'd prepared. The guest with a wedding ring on his finger.

"So what made you decide to take a whole week in Santa Barbara right now?" she asked, when what she really needed to know was why he was there alone.

"I wanted to get out of the cold."

She pulled his plate toward her. Stacked it atop her own.

How could a man who exuded such heat ever be cold? And how could she, knowing that he was married, that he belonged to someone else, still feel so compelled to be near him?

As their gazes met, held, as she couldn't look away because she wanted so badly to know every single thought behind the searching she found there, Marybeth blurted, "What about your wife? What was her name? Jenny?"

His blinked, and it was as if he left one world for another, but he still looked her straight in the eye. "What do you want to know about her?"

Nothing. Absolutely nothing. And everything.

And nothing again. He was a guest—albeit one who'd seemingly changed who she was. All these years of waiting to find a man who sparked magic—who sparked some kind of reaction in her—and he comes along married.

"Jenny and I…that's not something I can readily explain."

"I understand," she said, reaching for the coffeepot as she stood. She had to stop feeling things around him.

Craig's hand on the handle of the pot stopped her.

"Please, I'd like to tell you about her, if you don't mind. If for no other reason than because I purposely took off my wedding ring yesterday when I got here."

Danger, Will Robinson. A line from a drama space show she used to watch popped into her brain. A TV show from long, long ago. Pre-twelve years of age. Marybeth could see the robot's arms flailing all over the place, as though a precursor to what would come if she stayed in that room right then.

His wedding ring, wherever he kept it, had nothing to do with her.

"I don't think…"

"I want it very clear that I have no intention of behaving with anything but complete appropriateness while I'm away from my wife. I have never, not once, been unfaithful to her. Nor will I be."

The tone of his voice, so filled with emotion, as much as his words put her butt right back in the chair.

He had to be feeling it, too—this…whatever had over-taken her the minute she'd seen him standing in the foyer of her home. Apparently he felt it, and was trying to be responsible to it.

"I'm listening."

"I...Jenny and I are friends. Great friends. We hung out together in art school and were buddies for a couple of years before we ever talked about becoming something more."

Buddies with this man? Marybeth couldn't see it.

"We're good together. Good for each other. We understand each other."

At least he hadn't given her the classic my wife doesn't understand me line.

"There's mutual respect and trust because of that understanding. Most importantly, there are no false expectations. When both of us are free at the same time, we enjoy each other's company. But there's no hurt feelings, or longing to be together when we're apart."

"Then why did you get married?" God, he looked good to her. Even now she was hanging on his every word. Wanted to know everything about him.

"It was her idea," Craig said slowly, as though from someplace far away. "Neither of us had a lifestyle conducive to a traditional marriage. Neither of us wanted one. We're both the type of people who need emotional distance. Yet, we seemed to gravitate toward each other. Taking the next step seemed natural. Right. She was certain that we could make it work."

"What about you? Were you certain, too?"

"I wanted to believe her." He shook his head, seemed to come back to the present as he once again looked right at her. "I did believe her," he amended. "I wanted it to work."

Past tense? "And now?"

"I still want it to work." Craig toyed with the edge of his napkin, watching the shape he was forming as though it was some form of art. "I've never been in this situation before," he said, glancing up, then down again. His fingers were beautiful, art in themselves, as he worked on the soft paper between them.

"What situation?"

"Being in the presence of another woman…and wanting to stay."

Marybeth tried not to make more of his remark than was there. She wasn't for him. Wasn't ever going to be his woman.

"Whose idea was it to spend the holidays apart?"

"Mine, mostly." Craig continued to toy with his napkin, rolling, folding, forming something, all with just the two fingers. "Jenny's the daughter of French aristocracy. She was raised in a castle about a hundred miles outside of Paris."

Great, Marybeth was competing with a princess. But not really. She'd already lost. Before she'd ever had a chance.

But then, she'd learned a long time ago about the curves life threw.

"Her parents are stereotypically French. As far as they're concerned Americans are second-rate citizens. Most certainly not good enough to marry their precious only daughter. She doesn't pay much attention to their attitudes, never has, but she does love them."

His grin was laconic. "About as much as they don't love me."

"And that doesn't bother you?"

"I know it's not personal. They hated me before we ever met."

"So you have met?"

He nodded. "Our first Christmas together. Jenny goes home every December. They insisted on it as part of the deal they made with her before they allowed her to come to the States. Her entire family—aunts, uncles, cousins—shows up that week, no matter where they might be living. The holiday get-together is kind of a sacred thing with all of them."

It sounded lovely to her.

"That first year, I went with her. And decided never to repeat the experience."

"Why?"

"Because I hated to see Jenny so torn. She loves her family very much, and yet she sees what they are, too. The entire week, her parents acted as though she was alone. They never once looked at me. If they spoke directly to me, which wasn't often, they looked past me as if I wasn't there. I didn't much care…it left me a lot of time to explore France. I came home with more inspiration than I knew what to do with. But the week took a toll on Jenny. She felt terrible for the way I was treated. And yet she was pulled because that week is her only time with them and she wanted to be with them."

"Did she try to talk to them about it?"

"Of course. Jenny's not one to take things sitting down. But her parents think they know best, that their added years of experience have taught them things she has yet to learn. They keep hoping she'll come to her senses."

"So this isn't the first Christmas you've spent apart." She felt better. Less like a sinner. Sort of.

"No. And yes. After that first year, we decided to spend future Christmases with our respective parents. I hated leaving my mother alone and Jenny hated that the seven days she had with her folks had been spent in constant bickering over me."

Between his fingers an animal was taking shape. A body. Four legs and a blob where a head should be. A blob with points. A reindeer.

"She offered to stay home this year," he was saying, "because of my mom passing, but I know she misses her family, and they her. And who knows how long she'll have them?"

They both knew the hard truth within the rhetorical question.

"So," she had to ask, "do you love her?"

"Sure I do." This time when he looked up, it was as though

he was searching for something from her. As though he needed her to understand more than he was saying. "As much as I love, period."

"What does that mean?"

"I've just…I'm not a real emotional guy."

She didn't believe that. Couldn't believe it. Not with the charge he'd brought into her home with him. The man seeped from the inside out.

"How can you say you're in love and think yourself unemotional at the same time?"

"I didn't say I'm in love. I said I love her as much as I love anyone."

"Does she know that?"

"Of course. It's the same with her. Our passion goes into our work. By the time we get to the people in our lives, there's not much left."

The theory had merit. It was obvious Craig believed what he was telling her. And just as clear to her that he was one hundred percent wrong.

Which left her wondering—needing to know—why he had to believe it.

"When she's in the throes of creation, Jenny doesn't have anything left for herself. She'll forget to eat, to sleep, to lock the door if she happens to take a walk. That's where I come in. I make sure she eats."

Surprised by the prick of jealousy she felt, Marybeth tried to imagine a life with someone watching her back the way she'd watched her father's. And now her guests'.

Mostly she envisioned herself being irritated, feeling smothered. And yet as she pictured this virtual stranger there, concerned that she wasn't getting enough rest, strange things happened to her.

Dangerous things.

"Jenny and I are honest with each other," he was saying, "which is part of what makes us work so well."

She got that. And wanted to believe that his choices had no correlation with her life. She wasn't envious. She'd rather be alone than settle for less.

Wouldn't she?

"I've got to get going." Marybeth stood, gathering things carefully as she tried to put life—him—in perspective before she went down a path to destruction. "I'll see you later, okay?"

"Can I tag along with you to church?"

She'd told him the day before that she'd be going, offered to direct him to a congregation of his faith, if he attended at all. She'd not expected this.

There was something intimate about the thought of sitting in church with a man. Attending with him.

She liked the idea too much.

But it was Christmas Eve.

And he was alone.

"Sure. We can have something to eat around five, if you'd like, and go to the early service at seven."

"I'd like that."

She nodded. Watched him watching her. And when she made herself leave, she took the memory of his smile with her.

CHAPTER FIVE

Sunday, December 31, 2006

Will I always be as I am now, moving through life without ever being fully engaged? Is there something I'm doing that keeps me trapped? Am I sabotaging myself? Or is this the inevitable result to what happened when we were kids and a way of life for me that I can do nothing about—much like if I'd been in a skiing accident and lost a leg.

Putting down the letter, Marybeth stared at the handwriting through eyes blurred from lack of sleep. And maybe a few tears, as well.

Craig McKellips was gone. Finally. And nothing had happened. Oh, he'd helped her deliver Christmas dinner to the nursing home, visited with residents while she did the same. While she'd been at the Mathers's, exchanging gifts, on Christmas Eve day, he'd bought a miniature Victorian Santa lamp for the sideboard, had it wrapped and under the tree when she got home. He'd watched the original version of *Miracle on 34th Street* with her. Eaten voraciously and appreciatively all week.

They'd talked, incessantly it seemed at times, about the world, global warming and politics and same-sex marriage.

They'd exchanged long looks, and sat not far from each other on the couch.

And they never so much as shook hands.

He'd been gone for twelve hours—left that morning to make it home in time to pick Jenny up from the airport and spend New Year's Eve with his wife—and she was relieved.

No more pressure to save herself from disaster. No more temptation to want more than was her right to have.

But he'd be back.

In June.

She had a feeling she'd be waiting.

She'd told him to bring Jenny with him next time.

He'd said she didn't really like bed-and-breakfasts—preferring the anonymity of hotels. And room service available in the middle of the night.

He'd be coming alone.

His glance had promised her something she needed.

Craig had looked her straight in the eye when he'd stood at the door with his bag, having already taken care of his bill. Then he'd left without saying goodbye.

Dear James,

Putting the pen she'd been holding for more minutes than she cared to count to the paper in front of her, Marybeth didn't think, didn't analyze, didn't calculate.

As always when she came to this place, with pen and paper, no computers, no outside world, she was herself.

I've been thinking a lot about the questions you asked in your last letter. You wanted to know if you'd lost something vital because of what happened, if somehow your ability to love fully had been amputated. You seemed to think that I'd have answers for you.

I don't.

Do you remember when I wrote to you on my sixteenth birthday and told you that I wasn't dating at all?

I told you I was too busy. Playing tennis (a mostly individual sport), taking care of the house and cooking and laundry, babysitting Wendy next door, getting A's in college prep classes…

Well, you know all that; I don't have to repeat it all.

Then in college when you asked I told you I wasn't dating because there was no spark. Guys asked me out, they liked me, but I didn't ever return their feelings. I was fine to be friends. And nothing more.

Does this sound like someone who understands or experiences the fullness of loving?

Do I think what happened to my mom had anything to do with this? Of course, I do. And for you, too.

But do I think it's for life? I used to think so, but I don't know anymore. I can only tell you I hope not.

I spent my senior year in college fearing that I was going to be alone for the rest of my life. And the more frightened I got the more I became certain that I needed to meet you. I really believed that if we could stand face-to-face, if we could bolster each other in real life instead of only in this fantasy world we inhabit, we would be able to free each other from the binds that keep us hostage. Or, at the very least, to share the experience of being bound.

It took months for me to get up the courage to ask you to see me. And you said no. I don't disagree with your reasons. Of course there would be some level of awkwardness—at least at first. We know so much about each other that we'd never have told anyone we had to see again. And yes, life and society would intervene. Judgments might creep in. Maybe we would start filtering our words to each other. Maybe we would lose this safe place.

But maybe, just maybe, we'd finally be fully alive.

You ask about your lack of ability to love completely? Maybe this is part of it.

I don't know, maybe it's the holidays, my first Christmas without my dad, and I'll feel better again, soon, but I'm really kind of angry with you, my friend. I needed you this week. I needed a real flesh-and-blood friend. Someone who could cry with me. We're adults now, not kids.

I needed something more personal than your handwriting. (Although the familiar script still brings joy to my life.)

Yet you have a life I know nothing about. Very likely you're involved with someone. Guys don't live celibate forever. I know that it's not a mistake that the entire tone of our relationship changed since I pushed for that meeting. You backed away. We haven't spoken of anything personal to our daily lives in a couple of years. And while I love the philosophical discussions, while I desperately need what we have, this safe place to talk, to say anything and know that there will be automatic acceptance, I also think we're doing ourselves a disservice.

You are my best friend. My soul mate. If you're married, have a lover or a girlfriend…or boyfriend, if you have a child, I want to know them, too. Don't you see how crazy this is? I have a best friend who I know nothing about?

We've created something unrealistic here, James. The semblance of a perfect relationship. Anything real, anything here on a daily basis, grinding through the boring parts of life, would have to seem flawed in comparison. Wouldn't they? How could they possibly compete with total acceptance and support?

Look at me. I'm spending New Year's Eve alone with a pen.

Maybe we were both damaged by the incidences of our youth. Maybe we have had some vital part of our ability to give wholly and completely permanently stripped away.

Or maybe not. Maybe we have to end this fantasy to free ourselves to love in the real world. Maybe it's time we grew up and got over the past.

Please, James, can we meet?

Monday, January 1, 2007

My dearest Candy,

My hand trembles as I write this to you with hopes that it finds you well. Would that I could be there with you as you begin another new year. It's been almost three weeks since I sent my last letter and I still have not received one back. It's never been this long between letters and I hope and pray that you are well. I miss you greatly, my friend. I rely on your words, your presence in the tapestry of my life.

I need to know what you're thinking—that you are well.

As expected, the holidays were a struggle, though, as life would have it, not exactly the struggle I'd envisioned. As for the questions I asked in my last letter, I have discovered the answer. And I felt compelled to share it with you, lest those questions kept you from answering me for some reason.

I suspect, from things you haven't said, that you, too, find yourself unable to open up and give completely and I would hate to think that my ramblings and soul searching in any way made you doubt yourself. I want to give you strength, not take from you.

So…the answer. Yes, it is possible to feel deeply, to open up and give of self, beyond, or in spite of the tragedies of the past. I cannot tell you that the emotion is enough to sustain relationships as expected by the general population, but I do know that my capability to reach that depth still exists. This I can promise you with absolute certainty.

I found that out this holiday season.

I know, too, that you, that this very rare and special relationship we have here allowed me to risk going outside myself. I always had you, this, as a safety net— a place where I would be all right either way. If I could feel, then great. If not, well then, okay, too.

You know, one of the things that makes us so special is that there are no expectations between us. I don't have to behave a certain way, say certain things, do certain things, in order for you to feel loved and wanted. Nor do you. We just know, without thought or question, that, no matter what, we are there for each other.

Our friendship (such a stale, weak word for what we share) does not require any action other than an occasional pen to paper, so there is so little chance of failing at it. You know?

I'm not feeling eloquent today, but needed to get this off to you as the thoughts are raging through my mind. You are raging through my mind.

If I don't hear from you in another week, I'm calling the Santa Barbara police. I need to know that you are safe.

Happy New Year, my sweet, sweet friend.

As always, I am yours,

James

He'd sent the letter priority mail on January 2nd. She'd received it on the fourth. About the same day he would have received hers.

A very different rendition, yet on the same general topic. That's how she and James were. Aligned. At least in subject, if not in interpretation of the matter.

And she had her answer.

They wouldn't meet.

Friday, January 5, 2007

James,

Hello, my friend. I'm sorry to have put you through that last letter. Please disregard. As suspected, I was at a low moment—leaving behind the last year in which I would know my father, bringing on a new year of unknown. The holidays were rough, but as you always say, what doesn't kill you makes you stronger and I think I could now be a contender for the Olympics.

You are right. For us to meet would be a mistake. Expectations are unavoidable in the real world and I wouldn't ever want to disappoint you.

Or come here needing you and find you gone.

I hope that your dip into emotional living is only the beginning. I want that for you. And so much more. You are one in a million, James, a man who is loyal and true, caring and sensitive. Honest. Real. You deserve to have all of that in return. You deserve to have a lifetime of happiness.

I am well. Cared for. Protected.

And now…I have been thinking a lot about fire—you know me and my crazy, over-the-top analyzing. Anyway I read something about sitting in the fire with someone and I want to know if, had we ever met, you'd sit in the fire with me. I'm not really sure yet what that means. But I know I want it. Someone to sit in the fire with me.

Right now, you seem like the only one who qualifies—though, of course, this is only fantasy.

I suppose, to some, wanting to sit in the fire with someone could mean wanting someone to go to hell with you. But I knew right away that that wasn't what this author meant. My take on it was that fire was life. Living. In all its shades and forms. She wanted someone to sit with her, and she wanted to sit with them, as they experienced all that life had to offer. She wanted someone who was there when the going got tough. *That* was sitting in the fire. She wanted someone who loved her when she lost her temper. Who would listen when she sat and cried. Someone who was not afraid of her emotions. She wanted someone who would share their own intense moments with her.

Marybeth stopped as she heard someone come in the front door.

"It's me!" Grace's voice called cheerfully.

Calling out a good morning, Marybeth waited until she heard Grace getting supplies out of the cleaning closet at the end of the front hallway before she turned back to her writing.

Brutus, the traitor, removed his twenty-pound paw from her foot, scrambled from underneath the desk and loped out of the room to help with the morning chores. Or, rather, to supervise them.

Fire fascinates me. It draws me. And it repels me at the same time. I hate what fire does to homes. I hear about desert fires in parts of California and Arizona. The desert is so dry and the brush miles and miles of avid kindling. Then there are the forest fires that rage through

California, leaving havoc and lost homes and memories and death in their tracks.

These fires rage out of control. They're angry and destructive and seemingly all powerful.

And then I think about the movie *Castaway*. I watched it again last weekend. Remember all the lengths Tom Hanks went to to get a tiny flicker of flame on that deserted island? Without that fire, the warmth and the ability to cook, he was going to die. He scraped and rubbed and scraped and rubbed until he was bloody, but he finally got the fire going. That tiny spark of flame brought tears to my eyes. And throughout the movie, I hardly dared to breathe lest I blow out the fire. Snuff out a life.

I read books about life in earlier days, when people required fire to survive. Without fire they'd freeze to death in a matter of days. Or even, in some places, a matter of hours. Cowboys had campfires for warmth and cooking. Fire sterilized needles.

And today, when you're selling a house, you get more money if your home has a fireplace. It's a luxury. A wanted element. Fire speaks romance. Love. For centuries girls have gazed into fires dreaming. Books are written by the fire. Proposals are made, and accepted. Children are conceived. Or so I'm told.

Fire is one of the four elements in astrology. Fire, earth, air and water. Those born under Leo, Sagittarius and Aries are fire signs. We're bright. We're strong. We want to take control. We're the motivators. (Personally, my nature leans more toward water and air qualities than fire, but that's another story. And you, sweet James, are earth.)

This past weekend I was at a bonfire and I watched that hot, dancing light grow until those flames were shooting up past my head. The fire could have gotten out of control. There was definite danger there. My foot started to feel really hot at one point and I realized it was because the bottom of my boot was on fire. In seconds the rubber was burned right off. (Don't worry, my foot was fine!) And yet, minutes later, when I dropped an armful of wet brush atop that powerful entity, it languished. Suffocated. Died. Just like that. From a pile of harmless, limp tree foliage. A leaf couldn't hurt a thing. They don't fight back. They rip easily. Leaves are fragile. They die easily. Every year. And yet, the combined weight of those leaves killed a raging, dangerous power.

Feeling horrible for what I'd done—quashing someone else's fire—I had to coax the fire back. Tend to it. Feed it. I had to give it air. Fire, just like us, needs care to survive. And as I sat there later staring into the flames I realized that fire is a symbol for all of life. Just as fire needs air to survive, and can be drowned by water, just as it needs earth matter as food, nourishment, to burn, we all need each other, and the earth's elements. We all work together. Where I am strong, another is weak. But where I am weak, another is strong. We all have good and bad about us. Anger and happiness. We all can bring danger, or comfort. We all are a luxury and potential pain.

Fire is fascinating. And so are we.

Fire requires great care. And so do we.

You know, people teach their children not to play with fire. Yet at the same time, so much of the time we play with each other's hearts and emotions. At the very least, we disregard them. We take our loved ones for granted. Like my dad did me, I guess, and later, I did him, too. Maybe it wasn't just my mom's murder that kept us locked in our own worlds. Maybe it was me—and him—not tending to things.

I wondered, the other night at my friends' house, what would happen if we took that fire for granted. I figured it would do one of two things. It would rage out of control and burn down the house where I was. Or it would eventually peter out and die. When I brought that analogy back to life, and the relationships in my life, I knew the same would be true if I took them for granted.

I don't have answers to your earlier questions, James, but I do know that I don't want to disregard the fire. I want to sit in it. Until the day I die.

I wish you could come, sit a while. The flame is gently blazing. I'm tending to it for you.

Always,
Candy

CHAPTER SIX

Friday, June 15, 2007

Dear Candy,

No letter last week and you haven't missed a week since New Year's. I hope this just means that, with the summer season in full swing, you're too busy to write.

Please at least let me know that you're okay.

For the past few months, I haven't been able to stop thinking about you taking the blame for the distance between you and your dad. I try to see things your way, to assume that there is some truth in your statements, that perhaps you were closed off to him. But I have to tell you that I don't believe that's true. At all.

Remember last January when you talked about the fire? I just reread that letter. You said that the fire had to be tended to.

Candy, you did tend to your dad. To the exclusion of your own childhood a lot of the time. From the time you were twelve you were cooking and doing laundry, cleaning the house until he got the housekeeper. By your own admission, you didn't date in high school partially because you were too busy running a household.

And you didn't just run it, you thought about him all the time. You were trying to please him, to make his life easier. Better. You wanted him to feel loved and cared for.

Yeah, I get that your heart was frozen. But so was his. That was natural. And more his job than yours to heal for the both of you. You were the child. He was the adult. The parent.

It was up to him to teach you that it was safe for you to love. And love again.

Here's where we were different back then, and how I know that what I'm saying holds an element of truth. My mother didn't freeze me out. She didn't help me out, either, but she never gave up on me. Until the day she slipped into the coma, she was still hugging me every single time she said hello or goodbye. Still telling me how much she loved me. How much she believed in me.

She gave me a solid sense of self and that is the same thing that I've tried to give you all these years.

Lowering the letter to her lap, Marybeth took a moment to allow her emotions to settle, to blink away the moisture blurring her vision so that she could continue to read.

When she sniffled, not quite giving into the maelstrom, but not really beating it, either, Brutus raised his huge head, his hooded eyes peering up at her with, she was certain, concern. And question.

Smiling her reassurance, she tried to chuckle, and sobbed instead.

"What's the matter with me, boy?" she asked softly, her voice thick. "I haven't cried since Daddy died. I never get this emotional about anything."

Glancing at the notepaper again with the big bold JWM at the top—paper he had to have made exclusively for their correspondence as he'd had the name changed when he was far too young to have had personalized stationery—Marybeth sucked in another ragged breath.

And thought, for the fourth time in an hour, that she heard the front door. It was only one o'clock. Grace was gone for the day. The Grahams, who stayed in Jo's room, had left at sunrise for a daylong whale-watching adventure out of Los Angeles. Tanya Monroe, the number four slated LPGA golfer who was staying in Elizabeth's room while she recovered from anterior cruciate ligament surgery, was out for thirty-six holes of golf. And check-in for Jane's and Juliet's rooms wasn't until three.

Brutus didn't seem to notice any entrance sounds.

But then he didn't know that Juliet's guest was their holiday visitor. Marybeth was trying not to think about it, either.

If you don't believe another thing I tell you, please believe this. You are not at fault for your father's distance. You loved enough. You gave enough. You are enough.
   Yours,
James

The letter had come three days ago. Though she'd already responded to his previous letter, she'd written him back that night anyway, and sent the missive by overnight delivery. She didn't want James worrying about her.

And that's why she'd given him her phone number. He'd never asked. Ever. Not once in the almost fifteen years they'd been writing to each other. She'd never offered before, either, though she'd thought about it.

Still, he seemed to worry a lot more now that his mother had passed—as though the reality of death had only now hit home with him. Unlike Marybeth, who'd had to deal with that particular darkness at the ripe, young age of twelve.

She'd given him her number in case of emergency. For security. And peace of mind. She'd hoped…

He would have received the letter two days ago—if he was at home.

He hadn't called.

THE PALM TREES, more than anything, told Craig he was back in the familiar territory of his youth—home, no matter how long he'd been a resident of his beloved Colorado.

He thought of the sculpture he'd been working on in his spare time since Christmas. A seagull, flying on the waves, always touching. Never quite getting air bound. With all the commissions he'd had, he wasn't far on the piece, but it called to him.

As did the woman who'd inspired it.

Marybeth Lawson. She was like an injured seagull that insisted on flying in spite of the handicap, and didn't seem to realize that her feet weren't off the ground, that she wasn't getting anywhere.

Why on earth he thought he could help her, that he had the ability to help her, he had no idea.

But Jenny had recognized his compulsion to try. She'd been the one who'd pointed out the resemblance in the sculpture to his new obsession with California. She'd gone one step further, though. She'd thought he was having an affair.

As if he'd ever do anything like that.

He and Jenny needed each other.

QUARTER TO THREE and Marybeth was pacing between her quarters and the Orange Blossom's public entryway, certain she kept hearing the front door. With a bored look—he opened his eyes each time she returned—Brutus seemed to be encouraging her to sit down.

She did. At the Victorian desk in her private quarters.

The Vanderhoustons were going to be late. Way after seven. They'd called from Universal Studios in L.A. She'd already made up a welcome packet for them, complete with a key to their room, and stowed it in the box out front.

That left one guest unaccounted for that day. Another check-in.

She didn't go up and check on Juliet's room. Didn't put a welcome note on the dresser—as she sometimes did with returning guests. Nor did she add extra amenities. He was a paying client just like all the others. One of a crowd. Christmas had been different because he'd been her lone visitor.

She'd been missing her dad.

And the holidays were always hard.

And...

The bell out in the entryway tinkled and, heart pounding, Marybeth's breath caught in her throat. It had to be him.

Jumping up she faced the door out of her private quarters. Watched the opening as though waiting for a hand to appear and pull her through. Fingers clasped in front of her, she stood there a full three minutes and then, sucking in a long, slow breath, she walked slowly through the parlor and out to greet the man she'd been thinking about for months.

"HELLO! Craig McKellips, right?" She had an air of calm about her that had been missing the previous winter. The spaghetti strapped, calf-length cotton sundress added the sense of casual ease.

"Right." While he'd been filled with a sense of her for months, she'd become more distant, treating him as more of a stranger than she had the first time they'd met.

"Welcome back."

God, she was beautiful.

It wasn't the thought Craig meant to have as he set down his bag.

"Thanks," he said, ashamed with himself for the way he

just stood there, staring into those blue eyes as though he had a right to ask what was behind the polite hostess facade. "How've you been?"

She blinked. Glanced at the open registry book.

"Good. You're here for four nights, right?"

He wasn't sure what he'd been expecting—had refused to allow himself to do more than generically be aware that this meeting was coming. There'd been no fantasizing, no supposing—certainly no hoping. But he was disappointed anyway.

"Yes, that's right," he said, answering her surface question as he pushed his bag closer with his foot, moving in to sign the registry. "For the art show."

She might remember.

"Right. I've heard they're expecting record attendance this year."

Listening to her run through her spiel, reminding him about cocktails, confirming his preference for breakfast time slots, and telling him that if he wanted dinner reservations to let her know as early in the day as possible as places were booking up sometimes days ahead during this, the busy season, Craig tried to shift gears. To make this strictly a working trip.

"Don't forget," she said as she handed him the familiar set of keys to Juliet's room, "the front door is bolted at seven so take your house key if you're going to be out."

She glanced up at him. Fully. Stopped speaking. And he started to breathe easier again.

"Hi." He couldn't help the smile that spread across his face.

She didn't look away. "Hi."

"Are you going to have any free time during the next three days? Just for a cup of coffee or something? A few minutes to catch up."

With a glance down at his left hand—presumably at the

wedding ring he'd kept on his finger—she nodded, then glanced back up at him. "I'd like that."

Her voice had changed, grown softer, and far more like the warm, sweet, slightly vulnerable cadence he'd remembered. A vision of dinner followed by a late-night chat in the parlor—after all of her other guests had retired for the night—flashed through his mind.

Be careful, McKellips.

"I've hired someone through the show to cover my booth each day from one to two," he told her, picking up his bag to ensure his hands didn't do something stupid, like reach out to feel the softness of her cheek. "How about if you come over and meet me then? We could grab something to eat."

There was no answering smile on her face. "Okay."

"Or we could do it another time."

"No, lunch is good." He wasn't sure what to make of her quick response. "I always go to the art fair anyway…"

Good. Great. Phew. Okay. "I'll…see you…later then," he said, looking back at her as he headed for the stairs.

"It's the first door on the right."

He remembered. Every step of the way.

"Craig?" Halfway up the stairs, he turned as she called to him.

"Yeah?"

"It's…good…having you back."

"Thanks."

It was good to be back.

CHAPTER SEVEN

DRESSED IN HER favorite denim jumper and sandals, Mary-beth walked beside Craig along the thoroughfare crowded with vacationers and art lovers on Friday afternoon, patting herself on the back for remaining aloof—inside as well as out. They chatted about art. About the things they'd done over the past six months. About the rest of the upcoming weekend and the other guests at the Orange Blossom. Their hands never touched as they walked. Their shoulders didn't brush.

She bought her own lunch.

And left him at the entryway, telling herself that she was out of danger—over whatever hold he'd had on her. Lacking in magic once again.

She didn't see him that night.

On Saturday, Craig introduced Marybeth to several of the artists he'd met during his three years on the road, discussing their wares, the economy and the success of this year's show.

She learned a lot about methodology, materials and almost nothing about Craig. Except that while his peers clearly liked and respected him, none of them seemed to know anything about his personal life.

She pretended not to notice when he didn't show up for li-bations again that night.

On Sunday he showed her around his booth, talking about the

various pieces he had for sale, answering her questions patiently. And when she chose one to purchase, he refused to sell it to her.

She argued. He argued back.

It took her a full five minutes to realize he wasn't kidding. He didn't want her to own any of his work.

And that's when the numbness she'd been so gallantly wearing all weekend wore off.

HAVING SPENT all afternoon alternating between hurt, indignation, anger and a valiant attempt to believe she didn't care, Marybeth was waiting in the dimly lit entryway when Craig came in from packing up after the show at nine o'clock Sunday evening.

With a hand on either side of the doorjamb, she blocked his way.

"What's up?" His gaze was soft as he frowned.

Experiencing a brief moment of doubt when she heard the real concern in his voice, Marybeth nonetheless stiffened her backbone and stood her ground.

"Sorry, you can't stay here," she said.

"What?"

All of the rooms in Santa Barbara were sold out and the tired look about his eyes gave her pause, but not enough. He was young; he'd survive.

And he was petting Brutus like he was part of the family.

"I couldn't possibly take money from you," she reiterated what he'd said that afternoon. "You don't have to stay here just because I'm in business," she added, in spite of her self-avowal to shut up. "My rooms aren't good enough for you. Or, maybe they're too good for you."

When Craig's frown turned to a grin, Marybeth wilted just a bit. This wasn't supposed to be funny. For either of them.

He was supposed to get the point.

She was supposed to be making one.

Or something.

"What?" she demanded, trying for firm conviction while keeping her tone soft in deference to the other guests upstairs.

She wasn't going to smile with him.

"You have a temper."

That made her mad, too. If he knew her at all, he'd know that simply wasn't so. "I do not." He could ask anyone who knew her. They'd tell him.

Furthermore, she didn't like the way he was studying her, as though he could read things inside her that she didn't even know yet.

Adjusting the satchel on his shoulder, he glanced toward the parlor. "Can we sit for a minute?"

"Before you leave, you mean?" Though she tried to be, she wasn't completely serious. She wasn't really going to make him pack his bags at this time of night and try to find a place to stay in the bursting-at-the-seams-with-tourists town in the height of its summer season.

He didn't respond to her dig, damn him. Just led the way, with Brutus lumbering after him, into the darkened living room.

Marybeth turned on a side lamp. And shut the double French doors—just to make certain they didn't bother anyone else who might still be awake while she told him he had no right to be there. She'd long since turned off the piano medley of summer tunes that had been softly playing in the background for the guests that evening. A little noise, distraction, calming influence would have helped.

"Sit." Craig indicated the seat next to him on her favorite Victorian couch.

"This is my house," she reminded him, sounding, even to her, like some belligerent kid, and wondering what to do with herself.

She sat. A wadded napkin was on the floor beneath the

sideboard—something she'd missed when cleaning up earlier. A piece of trash she hadn't been able to see from a standing position.

"I'm sorry."

They weren't the words she'd been expecting. How in the hell was she supposed to fight with that?

"You have no reason to be sorry." What was it to her if he didn't want his work in her possession?

"I insulted you."

He was right. He had. But that wasn't his fault. She was one big overreaction where he was concerned. But he was leaving town in the morning.

Not a moment too soon.

Thank goodness.

"I'm the one who's sorry," she said, feeling more ruffled than contrite. "Of course you can stay here tonight. You've already paid for the room. It's yours."

For the night.

Then it would be hers again.

"Thank you."

"I had no business taking your refusal so personally," she continued. "Your pieces are all original. Handmade. Time consuming to produce. I can see why you'd need to save them for your collectors."

"I was at the show to sell that stuff."

Yeah. That's what she'd thought. So…

It started all over again. And though she saw the personal collision in her immediate future, she couldn't prevent herself from blurting, "Well, if you wouldn't sell to me because you didn't want me to feel obligated to buy just because you're staying here, then I don't want you staying here just because you feel obligated to since I went to your show. Or because you stayed here over Christmas."

Didn't he see the logic here? It was here, wasn't it?

"I didn't want to sell to you because I have a half-finished piece at home that's for you. I've had so many orders I had to fill, I just didn't get a chance to complete it yet."

Oh.

Well.

Um.

Uh-huh. The mortarless walls around her heart fell over in spite of the number of blocks she'd so painstakingly stacked there.

"I can't remember a time I've felt more like an idiot."

"Does that mean I'm allowed to sleep in my bed more than just tonight? That I can come back?"

His bed. In her home. That sounded good.

"Yes." Hands in her lap, squeezing each other so tightly they were tingling, Marybeth scrambled for sanity.

"Don't you hate it when you do that?"

"What?"

"Act out of character and then have to take it back?"

The flecks in his golden eyes seemed to reach right out and touch her. "It seems all I do when you're around is act out of character."

"Would it make you feel better to know that I'm struggling with the same malady?"

"How are you acting out of character?"

"I'm sitting here after a grueling three-day show instead of at a bar or in a hotel room with a drink in my hand."

"I can get you something…."

"Actually, one drink to unwind would be great, but that's not what I was getting at."

Jumping up, she crossed the room, stepping over Brutus at the entry to her part of the house. "What would you like?"

"Are you joining me?"

He was leaving in the morning. "Sure." One drink. That was all.

"Do you have vodka?"

She nodded.

"And orange juice?"

"Two screwdrivers coming up," she said. She heard bells ringing in her head.

Followed by a very sharp reprimand from the voice of reason.

"WAS I RIGHT when I assumed you were acting out of character earlier?" Their drinks were half gone and while Craig was enjoying her storytelling, engaged in her retelling of the more colorful incidents from her more than three years in business, including a baby who had been born at the inn since he'd last been there, he was also aware that time was gliding innocuously by.

And would then just be finished. Done. Used up.

The smile faded from her mouth as, wide-eyed, she stared at him, as though asking for help—speaking to something inside of him that could not refuse her.

"I ask because, as I said, I'm finding myself out of character, and would sure like to know that I'm not alone. And maybe even find some help in figuring out what ails me so that I can return to the regularly scheduled programming of my life."

That brought her smile back, if a bit tremulously.

"I… Yes." Where all the other sips she'd taken from her glass had been small, the one that followed those words was long. Deep. "If you must know, I don't do this."

"This?"

"Spend time alone with someone. One on one."

"Come on." If he relented, she'd be relieved. But he couldn't do it. "You expect me to believe you're always in a group of people? What about the lady that cleans for you? What did you say her name was? Grace?"

"Men. I don't spend time alone with men. Except my dad. Before he died."

Craig's muscles tightened from the inside out. "Forgive me if I'm being too forward, but I have to ask. Is there a specific reason for that? Were you…has someone…"

"No! I've never been attacked, or abused, if that's what you're asking."

"So…do you prefer women?" This was, after all, California—if a good bit south of the city known for same-sex lovers.

"No." Marybeth's chuckle let him know he hadn't offended her. "I'm an anomaly," she said without apology or any hint of dissatisfaction. "I like who I am and I recognize that I'm better alone."

"Are you happy?"

"I wake up every morning looking forward to the day."

Which wasn't quite the same thing, was it? Not that he was one to know.

"What about you?" Head slightly bent, she looked over at him. "Are you happy?"

Her directness, after a weekend of almost avoiding any acknowledgment that they'd even met before, was far too welcome.

He watched the ice bobbing in his glass. "Like you, I'm most content by myself. And…I find myself different than the guy I know when I'm around you."

"How so?"

"I can't think of anyone, other than Jenny, who knows anything remotely personal about me. Or me, them. And yet—" Craig couldn't not look at her "—I…think about you…wonder about you. I've been looking forward to this trip for months and I can't tell you the last time I really looked forward to anything."

Marybeth sat back, eyes glistening with sharpness, as though he'd scared her.

"Don't get me wrong," he added when he realized where he'd unwittingly led her. "I have no wayward intentions, no designs on your person."

He could speak with such conviction because the words were completely true.

"I just find pleasure in your presence. Odd, huh?"

Her eyes glistened as she shook her head. "No, not to me." Her voice had become a whisper. "I take pleasure in your presence, too. So much so that, when I think about it, it makes me uncomfortable. What's up with that?"

Craig sipped, and held on to his glass. Around her he had to occupy his hands. And watch his words. He couldn't lie to her. And there would always be things he couldn't tell her. "I can only speak for myself, but with me I think it's because you're so genuine. You don't play games like the rest of the world seems to do."

"Not much point in them, is there? I mean, if you're duplicitous, eventually the truth comes out and then not only do you have that to contend with, but you have the rest of the mess you created in the meantime. Besides, it's always seemed to me that people who play games with others, are also doing so with themselves."

Her words brought a twinge of guilt. Liquor induced. He wasn't creating a mess. He wasn't telling lies.

He was keeper of a secret that would only be damaging in the telling. It would be hurtful. And serve no good purpose. He held a secret that would go with him to his grave and the keeping of it, no matter how painful to him, would allow him to help Marybeth Lawson.

He was in control and fully capable of tending to her—and to his life, too.

He most definitely wasn't playing games with himself.

"Jenny knows."

"Knows what?"

"About you."

"What's to know?"

"That I was looking forward to seeing you."

The glass in her hand started to shake. "And?"

"That's all."

"What did she say?"

"Once she found out that my interest wasn't sexual, you mean?" No game playing here. He was going to make certain right from the beginning.

Marybeth's expression was blank as she nodded.

"Not much."

"Was she angry?"

"Not at all. You'd have to know Jenny."

"Maybe you could bring her with you sometime."

No game playing. Honesty. "Do you really want that?"

"No."

"Me, either."

"But doesn't that make this wrong?"

"For two people to share something asexually personal?"

"For a man and a woman to want to spend time alone together when one of them is married."

He wasn't going to buy that. He couldn't. "Look at it this way," he said instead, words coming to him before he'd ever really even processed the thoughts attached. "People who are alcoholics go to groups of fellow alcoholics to gain strength in the sharing of a common affliction, a common challenge. To find confidence in being who they are though who they are isn't society's norm, right?"

"Right."

"And some who've lost loved ones attend grief groups."

"Yeah."

"There are mom groups for just about every occasion, from being a new mom to dealing with puberty, older moms, moms of twins, moms of only children, stepmoms, empty nest moms…"

Marybeth grinned. He was on a roll now.

"You planning to be a mom, soon?" she asked.

God, she was gorgeous when she smiled.

"An ad for mom groups kept popping up on my Internet news site last week." He emptied his glass. And wanted more only so he'd have an excuse to keep her there with him. To stay downstairs with her, instead of being upstairs alone while their time together ticked away. "Anyway, the point is, sometimes people need the comfort or validation or support of being with others who know what they're going through. You and I, we both lost our only parent this past year. We're grieving and yet we can't talk about it. Don't talk about it. Because we're also emotional loners, which means that a grief group, where we'd have to put our emotions out there for others to hear, or even pouring our hearts out one-on-one, wouldn't work for us, right?" Craig kept talking, feeling as though his future rested on this soliloquy. "Being a loner and grieving is difficult because the first makes the cure for the second impossible."

Maybe he was stretching this. But he believed every word his mind was conjuring up.

"Think about it," he continued when Marybeth said nothing. "One who's an emotional loner wouldn't join a group. And yet there are times when we need validation, support, understanding, just like anyone else, right?"

"Like gravitates to like."

Now he felt like an idiot. She said in four words what he'd been trying to articulate for paragraphs.

"Right. We aren't man and woman coming together. We're like spirits recognizing our similarities."

Marybeth's nod was a get-out-of-jail-free card. Only much, much better.

CHAPTER EIGHT

AFTER SPENDING an hour with Craig exploring things they had in common—they both liked to read, kayak, in-line skating, take Internet classes, play tennis—Marybeth still wasn't ready to say good-night.

Good morning would come next.

Then goodbye.

"It's one in the morning," she told him. "I have to be up at six for the first shift of breakfast." Their empty glasses sat on the coffee table, where they'd set them after the first round, waiting for her to gather them up and whisk them away. She didn't reach for them.

"I should head up, let you get some rest." He didn't stand.

"There's something we don't have in common," she blurted as time stole away opportunity.

"What's that?"

"I sleep alone. You don't."

"I thought you said Brutus sleeps with you."

He had her there. Sort of.

"Besides, I sleep alone a lot of the time. I told you before about the erratic schedules Jenny and I keep."

The fact should not give her comfort. For any reason.

"Which do you like better? Alone or not?" She asked for purely clinical reasons. She hadn't yet had to share a bed on a regular basis. And had never been quite sure how she'd adapt to the invasion of what had always been her safe place away from eyes that saw too much, ears that would hear whatever tears the day had brought, minds that judged.

Part of her aversion to sharing her life with someone— apart from the obvious one of not having found anyone that she couldn't live without—was that her bed was sacred. A place where she could be completely herself, where her thoughts could run free, feelings could be felt in their entirety, and no one would ever know. Her sheets and pillows and mattress were her support, they were the arms that had been holding her in the dark since she was twelve years old and the pain had been too much to bear.

"Depends on the situation." Craig's answer was too slow in coming. He was clearly measuring his words and she realized he hadn't understood the clinical nature of the question.

She realized, too, that his loyalty was to someone else first, not her. Someone who shared his bed.

"I'm sorry," she threw out quickly. "I shouldn't have asked."

"If we were two men, or two women, you would have," he told her. "I just…it's going to take a little bit while we feel our way here, you know?"

How he'd so easily removed the awkwardness between them she didn't know, but just as quickly as she'd tensed, Marybeth relaxed again.

"Sometimes having company in the dark hours of the night is a comfort," Craig said when she'd thought they were done with the topic. "Other times it's not as easy."

"The same can be said for sleeping alone."

"And probably for living alone, too, I'd guess," he said next.

Probably. "I can't really say," she told him. "So far, I'm only here alone about ten nights out of a year."

But for all intents and purposes, when it came to bill paying, planning, decision-making, she was alone. Whether out of sensitivity or for some other reason, Craig refrained from pointing that out.

"You asked earlier if I was planning to be a mom," he said instead. "What about you? Do ever think about having children?"

"Of course I do. Everybody does at some point or other, don't you figure?"

"Yeah. Probably. With a few exceptions, maybe."

"I'd like to have kids someday," she added. "Not anytime soon. I'm only twenty-six and need to get the Orchard Blossom more firmly established before I even think about disrupting my schedule in such a huge way, but I think I'd be a good mom."

"I have no doubt about that." Craig grinned at her. "Just from what I've seen here, the way you nurture total strangers, you'd be a mom of the year."

"What about you? Do you and Jenny plan to have kids?"

"I don't know. We've talked about it, but mostly to say not anytime soon. We're not really the family type. Our art directs the schedules we keep—or maybe it's that the muse controls the brain. Hell, when Jenny's in the middle of a project she can't even remember to feed herself, let alone think about taking care of someone else."

His answer made her sad. She wasn't sure why.

"I take it, since you want kids, you have plans to marry at some point. When the right guy comes along."

She didn't. "Not really. No." She felt free to tell him, the same way she'd expostulated to James, who already knew her views on love and marriage and children. Grandchildren, too, for that matter. "Unless something changes, which is always possible, I'd go to a sperm bank. I'm not going to settle for a loveless relationship, or put a kid through growing up with one."

In her weakest, most lonely moments, she'd imagined herself asking James to be the donor—specimen sent medically through the mail. She'd had more than her share of those lonely moments these past months.

"Parenting alone seems like a hard way to go," Craig said now. "Doing a two-person job singly would bring a lot of challenges, but if anyone could do it well and be happy, I'd put my money on you."

Baffling though it was, the only thought that popped into Marybeth's brain at that moment was always a bridesmaid, never a bride.

HE HAD TO GET upstairs, to let her get some rest. If she'd only yawn. Or rub her eyes or stand to go. The minutes ticked into half hours, then hours and all he could think about was the six months in between this visit and Christmastime.

Jenny would be gone again. And if Marybeth would have him…

"You said that once Jenny found out there was nothing…well, nothing between us, she was okay with you coming here," Marybeth said as though she knew what he was thinking. Could the woman read his mind, now, too? Craig shifted on the couch, but he didn't turn from her.

"That's right."

"That kind of implies that at first, she thought there was something going on here."

"Right again." His nerves hummed.

"How did she find out about me? That I'm a young woman. I mean, you could have a sixty-five-year-old male innkeeper as easily as me."

"As flighty as Jenny is when she's working, she's also very perceptive. Which is what makes her a great artist. She picks up on the slightest nuances, senses things that other people can't see. And she also cares about me a great deal. As I do her. We're pretty in tune with each other."

"Why did she think you were having an affair?"

"She knew I'd met someone over Christmas and that I was going to see that someone again. She assumed it was about sex."

"Oh, my God, Craig. She could have left you! And because of me? I feel terrible. And…"

Feeling as though he were in the path of a runaway train, Craig grabbed her hand. "Stop," he said.

Whether it was his words, or the shock of their skin touching, Craig didn't know, but she froze.

And so did he.

He recovered first. "Jenny wasn't going to leave. That's not her way. And even if she had been, it wouldn't have been in any way your fault. If we ever split, it would be because there was something missing between the two of us. Period."

"But she knows now, for sure, that we aren't having an affair."

"Yes."

"Have you talked to her since you've been here?"

"Yes." Briefly. She'd been asleep the first time. And working the second. So Jenny. So expected. Predictable. Solid.

"And things are okay?"

"They're fine." Same as they'd always been. And as they always would be. Pray God.

"You said she wouldn't have left you, that that wasn't her way. What did that mean?"

He wished she'd leave it alone. Jenny and he were hard to understand. But they worked.

"Would she really sit back and let you have affairs with other women?"

Craig's thoughts were sluggish, as though suffering from far more vodka than he'd actually consumed. Or maybe he just didn't want to think.

"Other women? As in all the time? No. But then, neither

would I accept that from myself. That's cheap. And lazy. And selfish. If I wanted that, I wouldn't be married."

"But she'd allow a mistress."

There was danger here, in this conversation. In the possibilities it left hanging.

"She wouldn't be happy about it."

"But she'd allow it."

"If I was getting something she couldn't give me. But I still came home to her. Then, yes. She'd allow it."

"She told you that."

"Yes."

Marybeth's wide-eyed look bothered him, but he wasn't sure why. Because of the pity he thought he read there? Because of what he saw of himself in her eyes?

Or because she thought the tenor of their budding friendship was just changing again? He hadn't opened a door. Not with her.

Another woman, maybe, someday, would be okay, according to Jenny. But that woman could never, ever be Marybeth Lawson.

Even though he was only one of two living beings who knew why, he could never, ever be more than an occasional passerby in Marybeth Lawson's life.

More would beget more. And eventually she'd hate him.

"What about you?" Her lips moved, speaking to him. And for a second there all he could think about was the lucky bastard who'd get to taste them someday. "Would you be as understanding if the situation were reversed? If Jenny slept with another man because he gave her something you couldn't, but she came home to you and wanted to stay with you, would you be okay with that?"

"Yes." He didn't like his answer any better tonight than he had when he'd given it to Jenny four days ago.

"I could never do that," Marybeth said, frowning. "I mean,

it's great that you can. Probably realistic, even. But there's no way I could love a man, share my bed, my life with him and know that he was sleeping with someone else."

Craig didn't blame her. He would never have seen himself in such a relationship. And yet, with Jenny, it felt right.

"I mean, especially for a woman, sex is so much more than body parts. You give your most intimate self to someone else, you start to feel ownership toward them. You need them. You need them to need you."

Craig wondered who the lucky guy was. Or had been.

"Making love is the one thing that a husband and wife share that no one else in the world is a part of. It's what sets them apart as sacred to each other."

He couldn't imagine any man, ever, being willing to share her. With anyone. For any reason.

But he could imagine himself sharing his own wife?

The realization made no sense to him.

Monday, June 18, 2007

Dear James,
    I'm writing out of turn again, but I need to talk. I've been wrestling with a situation I heard about and need your take on it.

Marybeth's hand ached as it tried to keep up with the thoughts tumbling over themselves, crying for release. Of course, it was tired, too. She'd had an hour of sleep. Had served breakfast—three times. Then met with Grace to go over the plans for the week. They were taking roses out of the garden for all four rooms. And bringing in summer fun magazines.

They had a full house all week, but with changeovers in every room, which meant additional welcome baskets and magazines.

And Marybeth had said goodbye to a stranger who was also, oddly, a closer friend than most of the people she'd known for years. He'd said he was coming back for Christmas. And, for a moment, she'd breathed easier.

Until she'd realized a lot could happen between June and December.

He hadn't asked if he could call her. Hadn't asked for her private line. She hadn't given it to him.

She'd given it to James.

Not that he'd used it.

What do you think about the sanctity of marriage?

It's not really my business. I'm not married, nor am I contemplating getting married. And not that we talk of such things. But in this case, for this discussion, you need to know, at least, that I have no basis upon which to judge except observation, no opinions formed by experience.

I think marriage has to stand for something. At the same time, I guess it can be whatever any two people want it to be. It seems to me that the commitment involved when two people go so far as to legally join their lives makes the parties vulnerable to each other. The level of trust required to allow oneself to be that vulnerable to another person can only be given if one is relatively certain that the trust will not be broken.

And the only way to ensure that that trust isn't broken is to not step outside that one-on-one relationship and form close attachments with others of the opposite sex, right? How could a wife trust that her heart is safe with a man who has another woman as well as her? Isn't she, then, just one of a crowd? Just the one who shares the bills? The house, maybe?

What if she needs his help on a particular day and the

other woman does, too? Who does he go to? Where does his loyalty lie?

And what about that other woman? Emotionally she needs him as much as the wife does, doesn't she?

Or does she somehow feel less? Is there some kind of internal mechanism that goes into place when a female becomes the other woman? Like the instincts that I've always heard appear when a woman becomes a mother?

Is she wrong to be with the man when she knows he has a wife? Or is his relationship with his wife strictly his business? What if he tells her his wife knows about them? What if his wife doesn't care?

When the husband shares his wife with another man, which one of them is the one she turns to when she needs support? Or do they share her other needs as they share her body?

And, I wonder, how sacred is that bond? If a man ignores his wife, does the fact that she chose to marry him when he was a different person, a man who said he adored her, who wanted her love and adoration in return, bind her to him regardless? Must she now live out her entire life in an emotional wasteland? All alone? Is she sentenced to a life without touch and nurturing and companionship?

Or does she break that bond and move on?

If it's not till death do us part, then how does anyone have the ability to trust on the level required for wholehearted giving and receiving?

But if it is till death do us part, then what happens when living in the relationship is a hell worse than death? Or just plain empty?

What if a couple married, thinking it was best, then found out that they weren't happy together? What if one could be happier if they parted, but not both?

Is the bond more important than the individual's right to happiness?

And how could you ever give yourself completely, trust completely, knowing that any time, any year, your spouse could come to you and say he isn't happy and end what was promised to be forever yours?

Who gave any of us the right to determine these things?

In case you can't tell, I've been depressed today, my friend. I'm low on sleep and overloaded with thoughts.

But as always I feel better now that I've talked to you, given my wayward thoughts over to you for pondering for a while.

Thank you for being there, James. You mean the world to me.

I am always here for you, too.

Candy

CHAPTER NINE

Sunday, June 24, 2007

My dearest Candy,

I've been thinking a lot about your last letter. We've talked before about life being different for every individual. Heck, look at us. What twelve-year-old kids meet due to parental rape and rely on each other for the rest of their lives?

I really think that marriage, like life, is different for every couple, too. Just as no two people are the same, no two marriages are the same. What works for some, won't work for others. My take on this is, really, my answer to the last question you posed—who decides?

I think we do. Each of us, individually, for ourselves. We came to this earth with a mind to process stimulus and to think for us. With a heart and spirit to guide us. And with a body to carry out the dictates of the heart, spirit and mind.

We don't all like spinach. Or golf. We don't all want a houseful of kids. We aren't all good writers. Some of us are clumsy, some move with grace. And we aren't all going to want or need the same things out of the relationships we form in our lifetimes. Those relationships are driven by the individuals we are, so there isn't any one type of relationship that will fit us all.

The key to this, as I see it, is the responsibility each of us has to be up-front about our intentions any time we interact with others, most particularly if we're having an impact on their lives.

And the hope is that my intentions, or your intentions, jell with whoever is on the other side of the interaction.

Take you and me, for instance. I've been up-front with you about my aversion to us meeting. That aversion is more head driven than heart driven. I long to meet you face-to-face. Yet my head very strongly dictates that we risk losing this—the most incredible interaction I could ever imagine—and I cannot take that risk.

You, however, might be driven differently. You might need the meeting so desperately that at some point you choose to end our liaison because it doesn't meet your needs.

And I know this because *you* have been up-front with your intentions.

I think the same applies in marriage. If the intentions of both parties gel, then that marriage is the perfect one for those two people. Right? Regardless of how the definition of their relationship appears to others.

And if they don't jell, the choice to take the risk belongs to the risk-taker. And at least the risk is calculated.

Just my thoughts.

Love,

James

Wednesday, June 27, 2007

James,

I received your letter today. And what you say about marriage makes sense. I guess if I ever do enter into a close intimate relationship it will have to be with someone who is content with just me. I can't share. Not myself. And not any lover I have, either. This I know.

I notice that you didn't return the favor and let me know your marital status. I'm assuming that you're married now. I wish you trusted me enough to share the big moments in your life. You know, your justification of ruining our safe place might work for the whole meeting thing, but it doesn't fly for personal revelations. I'm not asking you to be disloyal to any relationships you have, or to betray any trusts, only to be able to share the daily goings-on of our lives like we used to do.

I miss hearing about you. I love what we have, James. It would kill me to lose it.

And I need more. From you. From us. Please.

Love,

Candy

Thursday, July 5, 2007

My dearest Candy,

All those years ago, when I read your profile and left my name at the center for them to pass along to you as a possible pen pal, I was thoroughly convinced that I did so for you. I saw myself as a strong young man taking responsibility for the evil men in the world. I wanted to be your strength. Your sounding board. I wanted to be there for you, without any idea of what that really meant.

And now, almost fifteen years later, I still need to be your safety net. Your unconditional friend and support.

But as I get older, I'm realizing that you are not the only one who needs such a friend. I'm fairly certain you never were. I feel like such a fraud as I sit here, facing myself. And showing that self to you.

I need you, too, Candy. You are my safe place. You are the mirror that shows me the things I cannot see in myself, but shows them to me with love and acceptance as opposed to the criticism through which I see myself.

Today, as I read your letter, I saw a man who was pushing forward with all-knowing, altruistic certainty blinding him to his own fears and shortcomings. I am finally able to admit—to you and to myself—that I have trust issues.

It's not that I don't trust you to keep my secrets safe. But I guess you know that already, don't you? My trust falters in the area of acceptance. If I give you too much of me, you might not like what you see and I might lose you, mightn't I?

I'm a coward. Hiding behind altruism. How long have you known this about me, sweet friend? How long have I been stretching your patience?

And may I beg for your compassion and stretch that patience a little bit longer? I will give you what you need, Candy. I will share my daily life in our letters. I just need some time to get used to the idea of a different you and me. To figure out what that means. To make certain that I don't hurt you or anyone else in the process.

Funny how, now that I realize that I've been hiding behind some macho idea that I was the only caregiver here so that I didn't have to give more of myself, I can see my weakness so clearly. Or not funny.

I feel as though I've failed you. And I'm sorry.

Love,

James

Monday, July 9, 2007

Dear James,

You could never fail me, my friend. Stop that kind of talk right now. No matter what we become, where we go, who we know or what we do with our lives, you are solidly here, a part of me.

You saved me, James, do you get that? You reached inside the dark abyss that was swallowing up a twelve-year-old girl that no one could find. You grabbed hold of me. Held on.

And when I was ready, you guided me out.

I don't care what color you are or how many warts you have. I don't care if you have six horns and are afraid of the dark, are gay or straight or drool when you talk.

I know you. The real you. The one who doesn't change, the one who you came here to this earth being and will go out of this life being. The you who will be in the next life, too. What do you think you've been giving me for these past fifteen years? I know about your loyalty, your compassion, your integrity, your attention to fairness and acceptance of other views. I know how you cared for your mother, in sickness and in health—even at thirteen, accepting her hugs because she needed to give them. In all these years, you never missed a letter to me. Not one. That speaks to the person you are.

Every opinion, every detail, every thought—they all showed me the spirit that is you. That was the beauty of us not meeting. You were very right about part of that. Your looks, your status, the way you move or the car you drive—none of them existed to distract me from seeing the real you.

Never, ever be afraid with me, James. Weak moments or strong, I see you.

You are safe. You are loved.

You have me. Always.

Candy

Monday, December 17, 2007

Sweet Candy,

Personal fact for today: Yes, I am married. She doesn't know all of the specifics of my past, but she knows that I have a pen pal from childhood. She doesn't often get the mail, but she's seen an envelope coming or going a time or two. She's never read a word of your letters, either from me to you or from you to me, has never asked to read them. She knows that I don't see you; that we've never met; and that gives her comfort, I believe.

I do not tell her what we talk about. She knows that my mother knew about you and fully approved of our liaison. She and Mom were very fond of each other and I think knowing Mom approved of you was enough to satisfy her.

There. How'd I do?

And now, I have to speak with you about something personal to your life. Something that I've been concerned about, on and off, for many years. (See what happens when you open Pandora's box? You might yet regret this, my friend.)

There's no easy way to present this so I'm going to say it right out. I worry, my sweet Candy, that you're letting what happened to your mother stifle your own sexuality.

I worry that your view of men has been so darkly

shaded that you cannot trust your heart or your life to anyone of my gender.

When you were in high school, I understood your aversion to dating. You were levels ahead of every one of your peers, and you'd taken on such a huge amount of responsibility at home. In college, I worried a bit more. You spent time with guys, but always only as friends.

And now you say you have no relationship nor any intention of having one—at least anytime soon. You're twenty-seven years old.

Human beings are not meant to live life alone.

You, sweetie, are far too caring and compassionate and nurturing to be happy forever without sharing your life in an intimate way.

Have you ever made love? Have you ever been able to let anyone get that close?

If so, and you truly are happier alone, then I must accept that. But if not, maybe you've got issues that need to be pursued. I take great responsibility here because by being your sounding board, by allowing you to vent with me, to speak with me, I made it easy for you to quit counseling.

And now I fear that you quit too soon. I fear that instead of helping you recover from that long ago tragedy, I have somehow made your way harder, your road longer.

Be angry with me if you must, Candy, but please don't disregard this letter. You have such capacity for joy, for ultimate happiness. Your capacity for giving and caring, for understanding is unsurpassable and what I know about life is that if you have that to give, it is also there for you to receive. Remember our talks about what you give out you get back? What you put out there comes back to you?

If there are unresolved issues, there are bound to be

some hard times ahead for you but I will be here. I will give you strength and comfort and support as you work your way through them. Always.

And to prove that to you, I'm including a card in this letter for you to keep in your wallet. It's got my private cell number on it.

If you ever need to speak to me, for any reason, use it. Anytime. I mean that.

Love,
James

The card read simply James Winston Malone, followed by a ten-digit number.

Sunday, December 23, 2007

CRAIG MCKELLIPS hadn't called. Not in six long months. Neither had he canceled. Or changed his reservation to include two.

Once again waiting for her sole holiday visitor, fighting the part of her that put too much stock in his visit with the more practical part of her that oversaw her happiness, Marybeth glanced again at what she'd come to think of as James's sex letter.

She'd answered him. Two weeks ago. And still believed what she'd told him—her choice to sleep alone had nothing to do with what had happened to her mother. How could it? She hadn't been at home. Hadn't really even understood, back then, what it all meant.

Except that her mother had been hurt.

And killed.

The card James had sent, with his phone number, was in her wallet.

He hadn't called her. Craig hadn't called her.

She hadn't called, either.

AT ONE SHE QUIT fighting the urge to check Juliet's room one last time. The sugar cookies were done—frosted even—and she had a full two hours before her one guest would arrive. Two hours alone. To pace. And upset herself.

All of the gifts for her friends at the nursing home were done. Packed in boxes. Ready to deliver.

She'd been prepared this year, more organized. Because she wanted to be free to spend time with her visitor?

She hoped not. She hoped she was simply one year more experienced. One year better prepared.

Grace had been in the day before to clean up after the last of the weekend guests. She'd left the room ready for Craig.

Marybeth went up anyway.

"This way I'll quit thinking about it and get on with baking the coffee cake for tomorrow's breakfast," she told Brutus as they ran up the curved, mahogany wood staircase. Or rather, she ran with him lumbering behind.

With his size, Brutus didn't have much more than a lumber. Or a heavy lunge if he was after something danger-ous. Like the mouse that had run through the kitchen a couple of weeks ago.

Everything in the room was fine, but she made adjust-ments anyway. Fluffed pillows.

Where Craig was going to be laying his head.

The big old house was quiet, slumbering at the end of a busy month. Maybe next year she'd have the money to wire the upstairs for music, too, so whatever she had playing softly downstairs would follow her guests to their rooms.

Just in the hallway.

Pulling a leaf off the poinsettia because it looked as though it might be getting ready to turn a little bit yellow on the tip, she wandered from bed to bathroom.

The towels hung evenly, side by side. Amenities filled the basket on the back of the toilet.

Running a finger over the refurbished porcelain that lined the tub, she adjusted the bath mat and checked that the middle drawer of the wicker storage chest still had a hairdryer. She'd had to replace a few over the years.

Back in the bedroom, she checked the floor for dust mites, adjusted the tie on the curtain—an important gesture as one of Juliet's finest assets was her view.

Craig's welcome basket sat in the center of the dresser, with extra fruit and no chocolate, and—

"Hi." The voice came from nowhere.

Marybeth screamed.

And kept on screaming.

CHAPTER TEN

COVERING HER EARS, closing her eyes, Marybeth screamed again. At the top of her lungs.

And just as suddenly, finally hearing herself, she stopped. Head bowed, hands still over her ears, she stood there, face burning, until she felt a human body close and looked up. Brutus sniffed her feet, her knees, nudged her hand.

"Hey." Craig bent, looking her in the eye, a concerned frown on his face. "You okay?"

Did she look okay? Sound okay? No, she wasn't okay. She was shaking. Had gone weak in the knees. She'd made a total and complete fool of herself.

"I'm fine." *Deep breaths, girl.* She patted Brutus's head when what she needed to do was grab hold. Squeeze tightly. "Welcome back, Craig!" She moved toward the door, talking to him over her shoulder. "Sorry about that. I was deep in thought and figured I was here alone and I don't know where Brutus was when you came in, but I guess neither of us heard you—"

"He greeted me like an old friend at the door." Craig was right behind her. "I got an earlier flight and thought I'd stop by and see if I could leave my bags here."

"Of course you can." Marybeth descended the stairs at a trot and positioned herself behind the registration desk as quickly as possible. "You can go ahead and check in," she added, still off-kilter as she grabbed the registration book.

"That way neither of us has to be back here at three." She could get the coffee cake done. And make extra for the nursing home, too. And for the Mathers. And—

"Marybeth."

She looked at him. And felt as if she was going to cry. Which was ridiculous.

"I'm sorry I scared you."

She nodded. Tried to laugh it off, but stopped when a sob almost escaped.

"Can you talk about it?"

"About what?"

"Normally when people are startled, they jump. Or let out an exclamation of fright. Not blood-curdling screams."

"I overreacted. I'm sorry."

"I don't want, or need, an apology. If anything I should be the one apologizing. I'm just concerned. What's going on to have you so on edge? Has something happened? Someone been threatening you?"

"No. Of course not." Starting to feel more like herself, albeit a stupid self, Marybeth returned her attention to getting her visitor officially signed into his room.

And Craig, bless him, let the moment pass.

THE FIRST THING Craig did after getting settled into his room was head down for what had quickly become his routine, welcome to Santa Barbara trip to the beach. The ocean, the sand, the fresh smell, the calm gave him a sense of homecoming he didn't usually find. Anywhere.

His hostess had reminded him she'd be serving libations at five. Until then, he'd promised himself not to think about her.

Just as he'd been promising every day for the past six months. So far he was 0 for somewhere around 183. Not one day had gone by without at least a passing memory of Marybeth Lawson.

There were three voice messages waiting for him when he got back to the rental car.

Dialing one, he waited to connect, typed in his password, wondering what Marybeth was going to think of the Christmas gift he'd brought for her. Hoping she'd be able to accept it.

"Hi, babe, it's me. I'm here. Just wanted you to know I'm safe."

He'd dropped Jenny off at the Denver airport the night before to catch her flight to Paris and spent the night in a nearby hotel, waiting for his own flight that morning.

"Hey, Mr. McKellips. Just wanted to say thanks for the golf club for my dad. It's awesome. He's going to love it."

A pro bono commission he'd done for a kid in rape counseling.

"Mr. McKellips, this is Amelia Butler from the New York Gallery…"

Craig took down the number from the prestigious art gallery. He'd been trying to get in with them for years. So why, when his chance might be on his doorstep, was he feeling more impatience at having to take the time to make the call than any sense of anticipation?

"MARYBETH, I think I'm pregnant."

Dropping into the white-and-oak chair at the end of her butcher block kitchen table, Marybeth stared at the young woman sitting next to her.

"Oh, Wendy." She scrambled for words that meant something, that conveyed anything. She took her sixteen-year-old friend's hand. "You think? What does that mean?"

"I'm pretty sure I am."

Focus. Be practical. She'd known something was up when Wendy had shown up at her door while school was still in session on this last day before Christmas break.

"Have you taken a test?"

Wendy nodded. "Twice."

"And?"

"It was positive both times."

Shit.

"Okay. Then you probably are." And now what?

"Have you told your mother?"

The derisive look in Wendy's eye said it all. "What do you think?"

Somehow between Wendy's twelfth and fourteenth year Bonnie Mather had lost trust with her daughter. The woman had always been one to panic too easily. And push too hard.

But she was a good woman who loved her daughter and wanted what was best for her.

"I'm assuming Randy's the father?"

"Of course! I'm not— This is me, Marybeth. You know me. I…Randy and I…we only did it once. Both of us felt horrible about it afterward and made a vow that we wouldn't do it again until we're married."

"And you've kept that vow?"

The cheerleader nodded, her sweet blue eyes brimming with tears. "It's been hard, you know? Mostly for me because I love him so much and just want to be close to him. I want him to need me that much."

"Sex isn't what you want him to need you for." That much she knew.

"That's what he says." Wendy's smile was tremulous.

"Does he know? About the baby?"

"Yeah. He suspected before I did. He's the one who bought the test and stayed with me while I did it."

Wendy had met Randy at church. They'd been dating, exclusively for more than a year—had been to the Orange Blossom several times, including an after prom party she'd hosted the previous spring. Randy had been so busy watching out over the premises, protecting Marybeth's property and Wendy's person, that he'd forgotten he was there to have fun.

"How far along are you?"

"Three months."

She'd be showing soon.

"What does Randy say about it?" Marybeth asked now, picturing the six-foot basketball star's reaction.

"We have to have the baby, of course," Wendy said.

"There are some good adoption agencies in L.A."

Eyes wide, Wendy shook her head. "I can't give up my baby, Marybeth. It's mine and Randy's, you know? A part of us. A product of our love."

Treading water so fast she knew she was going to sink, Marybeth gave Wendy's hand a squeeze. She'd been watching out for Wendy since birth. Wendy's unconditional adoration had been a daily strength to her at the time in her life when she'd most needed it. Somedays it had been only Wendy's sweet smile, her innocent love, that had brought her home from school.

She couldn't let the young girl down now.

"Does Randy know how you feel about the baby?"

"That's just it," Wendy said. "He wants to keep it as badly as I do, but I don't see how we're going to make it work. He wants to quit school, Marybeth. He says he'll get a job and we'll get married and he'll take care of me and the baby."

If anyone could do it, it would be Randy Pearson. She'd never met a more responsible seventeen-year-old. And the idea made Marybeth heartsick. For both of them.

"But I can't let him do that!" Wendy said, tears falling down her cheeks. "He's going to get a basketball scholarship." She sniffled and Marybeth reached for a tissue. "He wants to go to Cal State then on to law school," Wendy said. "And he's smart enough to make it, too. He wants to be a prosecutor and get the bad guys."

"You couldn't get married anyway," Marybeth pointed out while she tried desperately to figure out what to do here. "Not without a parent's signature. You're too young."

Wendy's eyes, still bearing a resemblance to the one-year-old baby whose tiny, chubby arms had wrapped around Marybeth's neck every day after school, were such a mixture of innocence and tragedy.

"You're going to have to tell them." Of course. There was no other option. Period. Not now that Marybeth knew. The Mathers were family to her, second parents.

Which Wendy knew. The teenager was shredding her tissue.

And all of a sudden, Marybeth understood.

"You want me to come with you?"

"Would you?"

Life seemed so simple—painful, but simple.

"Of course."

CONVINCING HIMSELF that he wasn't overeager, that he had things, himself, fully under control, that the excitement he was feeling was a result of the offer of a husband-and-wife show at the New York Gallery, Craig pulled up at the Orange Blossom at 5:05. He'd left a message for Jenny. What a Christmas gift for both of them. Odd. Marybeth's Expedition, a blue Eddie Bauer edition—not that he'd noticed—wasn't in the carport.

Stopping just short of calling out "hey, anyone home," after he jogged around and let himself in the heavy mahogany front door, Craig came to a halt in the entryway.

Two things were wrong. The room was empty. Not only was there no Marybeth, but no hors d'oeuvres, no libation, no sideboard.

And the house was silent.

Where was the Christmas music she always had playing softly in the background? It'd been on that afternoon.

And much more importantly, where was Marybeth?

The door to her private suite was closed.

Craig knocked. And knocked again.

Brutus barked. And barked again.

Was he early? Craig pushed up the sleeve of his sweater to check his watch. No: 5:10. Ten minutes later than he'd planned.

She couldn't have thought he wasn't coming and left. She hadn't had time to clear everything away.

Which left only one possibility.

Something was wrong.

Craig took the stairs two at a time.

"CRAIG?"

Standing at the foot of the stairs, Marybeth called up softly. If he was resting, or busy, she didn't want to disturb him. Whether or not he came down for cocktails was completely up to him.

She was to provide them. And she did. Every night she had a guest. Sometimes they were consumed. Sometimes not.

Still, she'd been late and—

"Marybeth?" The door to his room must have been open because he was in the hall without a sound. Frowning he gave her a once-over. "Everything okay?"

"Yeah." For now. "Sorry I'm late. I tried to get back in time but traffic's horrible—"

He waved off her apology. "I don't care about that. I…just…when I got back and you weren't here, I was worried that something had happened. I came up to see if you'd left a note. And was getting ready to call someone except that I had no idea who to call on your behalf."

Felt odd, having someone concerned about her. But nice.

Sort of. Usually folks just expected things from her. And she was fine with that.

Wanted it that way.

"I had a friend in trouble." She pulled the cliché out of a repertoire of them, except this time the words were spot-on. "Come on down. Everything's ready, I just have to pull it out of the fridge."

Craig fell into step behind her.

"If you want to wait in the parlor, it'll only take a second to—"

"You don't have to go to all the trouble of pulling the sideboard in if it's only me here," he told her. "And if it wouldn't be overstepping too much, I'd rather help than be waited on."

"No way." She shook her head, grinning at him over her shoulder. "You're paying me for this, buster. You're going to get what you pay for."

Craig didn't grin back. And she remembered how she'd felt when he'd refused to sell her a piece of his work, as though her offering wasn't good enough. And she remembered that it was Christmastime. And that he'd helped her through the second hardest Christmas of her life.

"But if you want, you could save me the trouble of having to set up serving trays if you'd like to sit at the table in my kitchen."

They'd be safe there. The professional kitchen she'd had put in with money from her mother's life insurance was in between the public part of the house and her really private quarters. The French doors leading into her small sitting room were closed.

She was pretty sure.

She realized, as they reached the door to her home, he hadn't answered. Turning, she glanced up at him.

Craig was studying her and she was afraid he was going to say no. That she'd misread. Offended. For a split second she was afraid he was going to tell her that he was leaving. Checking out. That he'd had a call from his wife, or someone else and had a better offer for the Christmas holidays.

"You sure you want to do this?" he asked instead.

Maybe, when she'd offered she hadn't been. "I'm sure."

"Then I'd be honored."

CHAPTER ELEVEN

SHE'D FLIPPED ON the music—a Josh Groban Christmas CD—and moved around the relatively small, but impressively equipped kitchen with confidence and an ease of familiarity, giving Craig his second sense of home that day. First on the beach, and now this.

Sitting at the butcher block table, he itched to get up and help her. Itched to check out the stove and some of the utensils hanging from the bar suspended from the ceiling.

He asked her about them instead.

"You like to cook?" she asked after the third query. Her brightly appliquéd sweater—black with a Christmas tree and presents—lifted as she reached for one of many trays from a slotted pullout in a top cupboard, giving him a glimpse of skin between it and the waistband of her black pants.

"I grew up with a working mom," he told her, focusing on the topic at hand. The only topic between them. "I learned my way around the kitchen early on. And I do most of the cooking at home."

Setting a tray of deviled eggs, veggies and dip on the table, Marybeth said, "So now I know how you learned to cook. What I asked was do you *like* to cook."

"Yes." He then confessed what only his mother and Jenny knew. "The cooking channel is one of my best friends."

Over the first glass of lightly spiked punch, Craig asked her about many of the dishes she'd served him, wanting her secrets, which she readily gave. And then some. He almost asked for pencil and paper so he could take notes.

"I'm a little intimidated now," she said, with the first easy smile he'd seen this trip, "knowing that I'm cooking for a professional."

Craig shook his head, chuckling. "Hardly. I'd be embarrassed to scramble eggs for you."

But he wanted to be able to sit at her table, sharing moments like this with her, for the rest of his life.

And maybe he could.

"This friend you went to help," he said now, comfortable with the idea that he could manage to be friend to Marybeth and loyal to Jenny at the same time, "is everything okay?"

"Not really." She looked beautiful even when she frowned.

"Is it something you can talk about?"

Taking a sip of her punch, she adjusted the celery on the plate, lining the little sticks evenly. Side by side. "I guess," she said, finally looking up at him. "If things go like I think they might, everyone in my life is going to know anyway."

Suddenly Craig wasn't so relaxed. "Why? What's going on?" She'd said the trouble was with a friend. Not her.

Unless…was there a man involved? Why he should immediately jump to that conclusion Craig didn't know. Nor should it matter to him.

"I was very close with my next door neighbors growing up. You might remember the Mathers, you met them at church."

"Bonnie and Bob. I remember."

"You might also remember me mentioning that my mom died when I was young…"

He remembered.

"Well, the Mathers kind of took me in as a second child. I was twelve years old and taking over a household and Bonnie taught me the things that I had not yet learned from my mother. Like not to put bleach on dark clothes. Or how to get soap scum off the bathroom tiles."

Heart faltering, Craig pictured her then. And ached, the food he'd been enjoying only moments before now untouched.

"They invited me into their family, taking me to the movies, on vacation, including me in Christmas parties, coming to school functions. They'd just had Wendy and probably the greatest thing they ever did for me was to share her with me. They'd pay me to come over and take care of her, even when they were home. I see now that they didn't need the help so much as they were giving me a sense of self, of life, of un-conditional love from someone who was full of hugs and joy and had no idea that tragedy existed in the world."

"What about your father? Was he okay with how much time you spent with them?" Craig would never have guessed that it was possible to be so fond of people he'd only met once.

"Oh, yeah. I'm sure he was relieved. I know he was grateful to them. They took good care of him, too, as much as he'd let them. We'd have Christmas dinner with them. Some years Dad would even come to Christmas Eve service with us."

"Did he go when your mom was alive?"

"Every year. He was on the pastor parish committee. But other than those few times during the holidays, he never went back after Mom…died."

She'd lost so much more than a mother. And there was no way to change any of it. To make it better.

"Anyway," she said, her tone of voice changing again, becoming more practical, more hostesslike. "Wendy came by today, after you left."

And she told him the rest of the story.

She grabbed a carrot, flipped it back and forth between her fingers. "The Mathers were hurt, shocked, worried, you name it," she said, "but they were kind, too. They never yelled at her. Or asked her how this could have happened. Or what she was thinking. They cried. They hugged her. They told her she wasn't alone…."

Had Marybeth had that kind of support through her adolescence?

"Is she planning to have the baby?"

"Yes. That's a given. It's just—"

At the curious look on her face as she broke off, Craig couldn't help but ask, "Just what?"

"What they're going to do with the baby that's in question."

"Her options are pretty limited at that age."

"That's what we told her. And her parents made it pretty clear they won't give their consent for her and the father to marry, but Wendy gets hysterical at the idea of giving the baby away."

"Would her parents help her raise it?"

"That's one of the things they're talking about."

Something was going on here.

"What other option is there?"

"For me to take it."

What?

"To adopt it you mean?"

"No. I don't think so." Looking bemused and lost at the same time, Marybeth stared at the table. Then at Craig. "I told the Mathers that I'd take the baby and raise it until Wendy and Randy are old enough to take care of it themselves."

"That'll be years."

"I know. But Bob's just been diagnosed with acute MS and is already in a wheelchair part-time. Bonnie's going to have her hands full with him. And stress escalates the disease."

Maybe so, but…

"You can't care for a baby from birth and then, years later, simply give it up." The idea was ludicrous. Suicide. "It'd break your heart into little pieces and…"

When her chin rose, Craig knew he'd said too much. And there was so much more he had yet to express.

His intensity was at dangerous levels.

"I've already told them I'd do it."

It took everything he had to keep his mouth shut. Filling it with food didn't seem to help. But he tried anyway.

"It's perfect in so many ways," Marybeth continued. From a glance at her he knew that whatever opinions he might have were irrelevant. She'd made up her mind. "Wendy will be able to be a teenager, not having to rush home from school to juggle motherhood and homework, but she'll still be able to see the baby whenever she needs to. I'll have a built-in babysitter…"

Choking on the cracker he'd just swallowed, Craig took a sip of punch. And forced himself to sit and silently listen. Maybe she'd talk some sense into herself.

Or see the error in the plan, the impossibility of taking on a child, loving it through midnight feedings and first steps, not to mention first words, to love it unconditionally and have that love returned, only to lose it all.

"It's the least I can do, after all they did for me," she continued. "Like that movie *Pay It Forward*…"

She saw too many movies.

"And it's not as if, when Wendy does take over, I'll never see the baby again."

"Unless she moves away."

"It'd be no different than any other grandparent and grandchild."

"Except that you're only twenty-seven and haven't spent years raising a child. You're not yet seasoned enough, tired enough, to be satisfied with grandparent status." So much for keeping quiet. "You've already lost so much, Marybeth, why take on something that is guaranteed heartbreak?"

"That's just it. I don't think it'll be heartbreak. To the contrary. It might be good for me. Look at me. I'm twenty-seven years old, as you say, and haven't had a date in more than two years. If I were going to be the dating type, the settling down to marriage and family type, I'd at least have had a date, don't you think? But I don't want to live totally alone all my life, either. Having someone else totally dependent on me, there every minute of every day, sounds really good to me. My whole life is about caring for people and letting them go. If anyone can do this, I can." Instead of saving her from herself, his words seemed to have energized the woman.

"Besides," she continued, "I owe the Mathers. And foster parents do this all the time—they take in babies whose parents are on drugs or maybe in jail but won't sign adoption papers, knowing full well that at some point they're going to lose those children either to a permanent adoptive home, or back to their biological parents."

Yes, but those people weren't Marybeth Lawson.

"The more I think about this, the more certain I am that I want to do it." Her gaze was clear, open—and more eager than Craig had seen it.

"What about the baby?" he tried once more, in spite of his certainty that he was fighting a losing cause.

He just couldn't convince himself that Marybeth's choices were none of his business.

"What about it?"

"It spends the first two to six years thinking you're its mother, relying on you, bonding with you. How do you explain to him or her that you're only temporary? That he or she can love you, need you, but eventually it'll only be from a distance?"

"Wendy will be around, loving him, too," she said. "And Randy. And the Mathers, and Randy's parents, too, I'm sure. Children are resilient. As long as people are there, loving them, they adapt. I know that from experience. We have such a stereo-typical definition of families in this country—you know, Mom, Dad and the kids. But in truth almost half the kids in America grow up with some other definition whether their parents are divorced or never married, or one or both are deceased."

He couldn't argue with that. Really, had no business arguing at all. "Foster parents generally don't have only one child." He threw that out there for no reason other than that he couldn't shut up, couldn't let this go. "And they don't have them for years. The baby might be fine—probably will be fine, with all the family you describe. Hell, it might be the luckiest little guy—or girl—alive, but you're still left in the cold. You spend the next several years raising someone else's child, what happens to your chances of meeting someone, having a family of your own?"

The ease with which she shrugged off his words didn't bode well. "They can't get any worse than they are now," she said with a twisted grin. "I don't have all the answers. I've only had a few hours to digest the whole thing. But I know that no matter what, I'll survive just fine. I always do."

And that's what concerned him most.

She knew how to survive, but did she know how to live?

CHAPTER TWELVE

SHE DIDN'T SLEEP WELL. As a matter of fact, Marybeth hardly slept at all. Sometime in the middle of the night she'd gotten up to write to James, but, while she'd sat at her desk, gathered paper and pen out of the drawer, she'd been unable to find words past *Dear James.*

Would he, like Craig, think she was making a mistake?

Her thoughts wouldn't focus. Her mind wouldn't be still.

If she was going to have a baby in her home, she'd have to make some changes. A lot of changes. By June.

Craig was upstairs. Sleeping in one of her beds. She'd invited him in to her private quarters. Sort of. He'd only been in the kitchen, but still, she'd allowed a guest to cross the threshold between the parlor and her area of the house. She could count on one hand the people she let into her space.

Being a hostess was great. Fun sometimes. Rewarding most of the time. Her job allowed her to interact without risking her heart. And kept a very clear boundary around her.

But what happened now that someone had crossed that line?

And then there was Wendy.

Dear, sweet Wendy. This was going to be a Christmas she'd never forget. And not because Santa brought her what she wanted.

Craig didn't approve of her choice to raise Wendy's baby. Was he right?

If she had the baby, would he return in June?

Would he be there when she was learning how to be a mom? Toting a baby while she went about her work.

She'd let him get too close. Couldn't care about his opinion. He was a visitor. One of hundreds. Nothing more.

Him being in her kitchen meant nothing. Changed nothing.

He'd been a perfect gentleman when he'd said good-night. Hadn't touched her.

Problem was, she'd wanted him to.

WHEN THE ALARM went off, Marybeth rolled over, certain that she'd just fallen asleep. She got up anyway. Made breakfast. She set the table with floating poinsettia candles and linens and the Christmas china. Piped the Christmas music throughout the downstairs. Prepared for the list of things she had to do before Christmas Eve service. Wrapped the gift she'd bought for Craig, hiding it under the tree in the parlor. And stumbled through it all only half aware of that which she did.

Would having the baby in her life cure her of her inexplicable, inappropriate and dangerous fascination with her married holiday visitor?

She should never have invited Craig into her kitchen. She'd known better. If only she hadn't had such an emotionally charged day…

If only she hadn't felt so drawn to him long before he'd ever stepped foot near her private door.

Not that that mattered. He was married. And by next year at this time, if the Mathers chose to take her up on her offer, she'd have a six-month-old baby. A load of presents under the tree that would stay and be opened. A reason to get up at the crack of dawn on Christmas morning to see the awe in little eyes as they surveyed what Santa brought.

Maybe. It might be the year after before her borrowed son or daughter would be old enough to appreciate a present.

A year. Maybe it would take two. How old were kids when they really got Christmas? Would she still have the child by then?

Upon that question, came another.

Would she really be able to survive giving the baby back?

SHE SURVIVED the day. Finished all of the last-minute cooking, delivered fifteen pounds of her signature dressing to the nursing home, picked up the fresh turkey for Christmas dinner for her and Craig the next day, talked to an aching-hearted Bonnie Mather for over an hour, refused three more last-minute invitations for parties and Christmas Day dinners, dropped off sugar cookies to some of her neighbors from the old neighborhood and at church for the social after early service that evening, went up to make the bed and clean the bath in Juliet's room only to find that her guest had already done so, fed Brutus—could she keep him with a baby in the house—and stayed out of Craig McKellips's way.

Until that evening when he knocked on the door of her private quarters at 5:10—ten minutes after she'd laid out his evening snacks and hurried away.

"Are you joining me?"

The once-over he gave her, up and down the black jeans twice, made her hands shake.

"I don't think that's a good idea." She'd chosen the red sweater with the appliquéd and sequined manger scene on purpose. To remind her what mattered at the end of the day. Family. Babies. Responsibility.

His frown was hard to take, as was the disappointment he didn't bother to hide. "Why?"

"I just…right now…I don't think it's a good idea."

"If that's how you really feel, then…okay." His face settled into an impassive look she'd never seen before.

That was it. He'd gotten the message. Didn't argue.

Turn around. Shut the door.

She turned around.

"It's not you." She didn't mean the words to slip out. Or to stand there. With all of her heart, she didn't mean to turn around. To meet that golden-eyed gaze.

He'd dressed up—a pair of black chinos, red button-down shirt beneath a black sweater with the longish blond hair dancing with the collar—a sight she'd never forget.

"Well that's good," he said, his hands in his pockets, "because I can tell you, I never mind losing a friendship as long as I know it's not my fault."

"I—" She stopped. Stared. "You aren't— We're still friends." If that's what you called this strange whatever they shared twice a year.

"So what's the problem?"

Oh, God. *Keep your mouth shut, Lawson. Firmly, completely shut.* She held her tongue with her teeth. Tasted blood.

And let go. "I don't know." The words came tumbling out.

"Can we talk about it?"

Could she stop herself? Did she have any say at all where he was concerned? "I guess."

And for what purpose? There were no answers to seek. Nothing to be gained save, perhaps, further humiliation.

Is that what he was, then? A strong nudge to her to be more humble?

She poured wine. Two glasses. Without asking him if he wanted any. She needed some and didn't drink alone.

She filled a plate—relieved when he followed suit.

She sat.

"I'm— You're— I—" She couldn't do it.

"You're what?"

"Not hungry."

Jutting out his chin, he studied her. Took a bite of a chipped beef-smeared pita.

"Mmm," he said, swallowing. "Another great recipe."

"My mother's."

He took another bite. "So what are you, besides not hungry?"

"You don't let a person off the hook, do you?"

"Not usually."

"Why is that?" She sipped. And sipped again. She'd love to empty the glass. Or the bottle. Pass out. And wake up herself again.

"Generally speaking, it's when someone wants to escape that they most need to stay. And whatever they're avoiding telling me is something I most need to hear."

"Like when your wife told you that you could sleep with someone else as long as you went back to her—stayed with her?"

She hadn't just said that, either. Okay she had. And she was going to get over this. Once and for all.

"You do things to me, Craig." She delivered her message with more authority than warmth. "I don't like them. I don't want them. And until I can figure out how to obliterate them, or, God willing, they simply go away, I have to keep my distance from you."

Leaning down to his plate, Craig froze. Then slowly straightened—without food.

"What things?"

What did that matter? Didn't he hear her? She was getting rid of them. One way or another.

"I…" Had absolutely no idea what to say.

"Please, Marybeth. I need to know. It's important."

"Why?"

"Because I feel…things…too."

CRAIG DROVE HER to church. Sat with her during the service, singing familiar hymns, half listening to the age-old story of the birth of Christ, lighting his candle from hers at the appropriate time. He withstood the looks from almost everyone in the small congregation. For the second consecutive year. With her.

And heard her explain, half a dozen times, that he was a guest at the inn. That he had no family in the area. Nowhere to go.

Smiling his way through the sympathetic nods and merry wishes, he was glad to finally escape to the rental car.

And took off as soon as Marybeth had her door shut.

"Where are we going?" she asked about two minutes into the drive.

"The beach."

"Why?"

"Because we need to talk and that's the best place I can think of."

Somewhat heartened when she didn't argue, Craig spent the rest of the drive asking for divine help for the upcoming conversation. Assistance from angels who'd lived on earth before, who understood him and his conflicts.

"Do you want to walk?" he asked as soon as he'd parked along the road.

"Okay."

Without touching they traversed the grassy area between the road and the beach. Marybeth's boots were low heeled enough for walking on the sand and he led them as close to the ocean as he could get without danger of wrestling with incoming waves.

"Let me know if you get too cold."

She nodded.

"We can't leave the situation as we did back at the house."

The first words came easy. They'd been repeating in his brain all through church.

He thought she nodded again, but couldn't be sure.

"We have to talk about what we're feeling. And more importantly, what we are and are not going to do about it."

"I agree."

Good. Fine.

"These…things…you're feeling. Can you be a little more explicit?"

"No."

Okay. That was fair.

"But you'll admit, there's something here. Between us."

"What do you mean by that?"

"We're drawn to each other."

When she lagged behind, he realized he'd been power walking. On sand. He slowed his step. "I guess," she said.

"You guess." She guessed? Then maybe they didn't have a problem after all.

"I…yeah, you're right."

He'd thought so. And while a very small part of him gloried in her response, the rest of him, the majority of him, wished the truth were different.

"And that's okay," he told her. "We talked about this last year. There's nothing wrong with us being friends."

"Right."

"So why were you avoiding me tonight?"

This time she missed a step. The blood heated in his veins…and someplace else that shamed him. Dammit to hell. He wasn't going to blow this. He was going to be a better man than the one who'd sired him.

"I'm…I find you…I'm attracted to you." The words were delivered with a tone of despair.

Houston, we have a problem.

But one they could handle. They simply had to get a handle on it. That was all. Craig was certain about that.

"I think about you too much."

His body tightened. They just had to tend to this and everything would be fine. Tend to it quickly.

"Sometimes, when you're around, I don't even recognize myself."

Stop. He had to stop her. So they could tend to it.

"This would all be a little less painful if you'd say something."

"I'm married."

CHAPTER THIRTEEN

IF MARYBETH had ever scripted her emotional demise, it wouldn't have been as bad as that moment on the beach.

Craig's words continued to reverberate in her head, as she searched for an inch of pride to salvage. She'd misread him. Thought, probably because she was so far gone, that he'd been attracted to her, too. That he'd understood what she'd been talking about earlier at the house, that he'd known what he was saying to her when he'd said he felt things, too.

Not that she'd intended them to do anything about their burgeoning desire—too strong a word but she couldn't come up with another. Whether he and his wife were okay with extramarital affairs or not, she absolutely was not.

"I know you're married." They were the only words she could manage to drop into the silence.

"I didn't manage that very well."

"No, you did fine."

He stopped, turned to face her, his eyes glistening in the moonlight, his hands in his pockets. "No, I didn't. What I was trying to avoid saying—the complete truth—is that I'm attracted to you, as well. Very much so."

Oh. Those little, unfamiliar swirls that had started in her intimate regions the night before, returned.

"But that doesn't mean that I intend to take advantage of you, or your feelings."

She wanted to tell him that he needn't worry. She wouldn't have allowed him to get close to that. Where were words when she needed them?

"I also don't want it to ruin our friendship," he continued and from some small place, a hint of peace entered Marybeth's heart. "My life is complicated," he told her, and she knew that, with him, the words weren't a brush-off of any kind.

In accord, they started to walk again, in spite of the fact that they were already several blocks from where they'd left the car. "I love Jenny." His voice dropped, coexisting with the lapping waves, rather than battling them. "I'm not *in love* with her and I don't think she's in love with me, either. But what we have—it works. It's what we both want."

"I have no intention of coming between the two of you. Ever."

"I know that," he told her and, though she could feel his gaze on her, she continued to watch the sand for any moving shadows.

"But even if there was no Jenny, I wouldn't start something with you."

Ouch. Breath catching in her throat, Marybeth concentrated on not tripping a third time.

"And that didn't come out how I intended, either," he said, offering a bit of salve to a wound she'd only begun to feel.

"You're an incredible woman, Marybeth. A giver. A nurturer. I'd never be able to give you the depths of love and commitment that you need. No matter how hard I tried to do otherwise, I'd end up hurting you. And hating myself."

It was a good thing she'd held out no hope for anything between the two of them. His sincerity would have dashed it.

"Sounds like you know yourself pretty well," she told him, even as she understood. He could have been talking about her. If he'd known her better.

"What I know," he said, stopping again, facing her, "is that this bond between us, it's rare. And important. I believe we can find a way to be together without compromising our selves, or each other. We have to keep things in the open and we'll be fine."

For the first time since she'd let him into her apartment the night before, Marybeth's heart settled. "I'd like that."

"I think if we stop fighting this thing, quit ignoring it, or trying to convince ourselves it doesn't exist, and just accept it, just as we accept that we will never act upon any physical connection that might accompany our friendship, we could have a lifetime relationship ahead of us."

God, she hoped so.

More than anything—other than that James would relent and meet her—she hoped so.

RELIEVED of one of the greatest burdens he could ever remember carrying, Craig didn't want this Christmas Eve to end. He and Marybeth had walked a couple of miles talking about Christmases past, sharing memories of easier times before turning around and still had another mile or so to go before they were at the car. It had to be close to midnight. And he wasn't the least bit tired.

He wanted to take her hand, but satisfied himself with knowing that, if things were different, she'd want that, too. Knowing that it was okay for him to want such things.

It was okay to feel them.

Just not act on them.

Probably one of the best Christmas presents he'd ever received.

"CAN I ASK YOU something?" Craig was so close she could feel his heat and still, he didn't so much as brush her hand.

Free from the constrictions attraction had placed on her—fear of where the attraction would lead—she said, "Sure," without really even thinking about her response.

They were just friends. Kind of like her and James only their conversations weren't on paper.

"That scream yesterday when I arrived, what was its source?"

She'd forgotten about that.

"I'd really like to know." His voice was calm in the night. Reassuring in the darkness.

Maybe it was the church service. Maybe it was the strength of the ocean.

Or maybe it was the fact that Marybeth was feeling a deep, personal, one-on-one connection with Craig.

Maybe she was just so damned relieved that she wasn't going to lose him, that she was safe with him, in spite of herself.

Whatever the reason, when she waited for the walls to shoot up, to shut her off from him, they didn't appear. When she tried to answer him, she could.

"I used to have these nightmares." Even James didn't know about them. Because there were some things she'd never told anyone. Some things she'd had to not talk about.

"I'm at home, in my living room. I'm young. Twelve or so." Her voice was distant enough, held by the air and the ocean, that its sound didn't scare her away. "This man comes in. I know he's going to hurt me. I can't quite figure out how, but I know that I'll never be the same again. I scream and scream and scream, but it doesn't help. He doesn't go away. It's like he can't hear me."

After yesterday's scare, she'd been afraid to sleep last night, lest he come again.

One foot in front of the other. She would get up the beach that way. And through life, too.

"The next thing I know there's this huge puddle of blood

on the floor, beside the couch. I start to cry and I know I'll never stop."

But she did stop. Years ago. She was okay now. He couldn't hurt her again.

Mostly lost in long ago times, Marybeth didn't realize the silence was stretching out for so long until Craig spoke.

"Then what happens?"

"I wake up." In the early days, she'd be sobbing.

"That's it. You don't see anything else?"

"That's it. And that's also the first time I've ever told anyone about it."

"You're kidding, right?" And yet, she knew he knew she wasn't. His tone was more commiseration than question. "Was this before or after your mother died?"

"After." They had the beach to themselves this Christmas Eve and as a December breeze blew over the ocean, she shivered, in spite of the heavy sweater she was wearing.

"So what about your dad? Or the Mathers?"

"I didn't tell them."

"Not even when you first woke up? You didn't call out?"

"Sure." She shrugged, shoulders hunched against the sudden chill. "But Dad was a sound sleeper. He never heard."

"So why not go to him? Surely he'd have wanted to know."

Some things weren't explicable. "He was hurting, too." She tried anyway. "I didn't want to add to his troubles. And after the first time or two I knew I could deal with them on my own. It was only a dream. I knew, as soon as I woke up, that it would fade."

"Helping you probably would have helped him."

Maybe. Probably. "He was so sad all the time and I guess I was afraid that if I was a problem, he'd ship me off or something…"

But she hadn't realized that then, either. Or even had the

thoughts in any concrete fashion before this moment on the dark beach.

With a friend by her side, Marybeth allowed her mind to wander back, to take a peek at things long buried.

"Can you tell me how your mother died?"

She slowed. Lost her breath. And kept on walking.

You should've seen the question coming. You opened a door. You know better than to open that door. To anyone.

"I don't…" *talk about that. Everyone knows better than to ask. Don't ask. Take the question back, Craig.*

"I'm not sure." Reaching deep inside herself, she tried. "I never have." Not in counseling. Not with James. No one had pushed. They'd all told her to take her time. To talk when she was ready.

She'd never been ready.

Hands in his pockets, Craig slowed their pace more. "Take your time."

Words she'd heard so many times before. Words that, always before, had been her escape route. So why wasn't she shutting down?

Marybeth truly did not understand herself. Didn't understand what was happening. Why this man in particular was different than anyone else she'd ever met. As though, in some weird way he was hers. Part of her.

Being with him was like being with a part of herself that she'd just met.

"I was twelve." She'd already said that. It was a way in. Maybe.

"The day started like any other. Nothing stands out. She woke me up with her usual 'Good morning, sunshine' at my door."

Sunshine. Her mom had called her sunshine. How could she possibly have forgotten that?

"I went to school. I heard that I'd been chosen to represen our junior high in some home ec something or other."

She'd forgotten that, too. Disoriented, Marybeth continued this nighttime beach tour taking on a twilight zone hue.

"Did you do well?"

"I don't know. I don't remember. I don't think I did it." S many chunks of that time were gone. Because she'd pushed them away for so long they'd faded away? Like her ability to bring her mother's face into clear focus?

"I remember walking home from school, being excited to tell my mom about it. It had to do with some recipe o dessert I'd made."

"So you were a good cook even then."

"I guess. Maybe my mom made it."

"You wouldn't have been asked to represent your schoo if your mom made it."

"I guess you're right." But it was only a guess.

"The next thing I remember is coming around the corne and seeing a ton of flashing red lights up and down our street Vehicles were everywhere, and at first I thought something was wrong with the road. You know, a crash or a fire or a leah or something."

That vision hadn't faded. It was as though she was there red lights flashing. Shaking her head, Marybeth tried to focus The darkness, waves swishing against the sand, all seeme foreign against the cacophony of sound and brightness s extreme it hurt her head and burned beneath her eyelids.

She stumbled.

"Slow down."

She heard his voice, but couldn't see through the haze, residual of flashing lights. "Marybeth, don't walk so fast. It' okay. I'm right here with you."

The voice had no effect on her. Of course people were there

with her. They were everywhere. Talking to her. Mostly men. Trying to hold her back. Calling for someone to "get the kid out of here."

They were at her house. All the cars and trucks. A fire truck. Some ambulances. Police cars. Other cars. Her mom's car. Not her dad's. People were all over the grass. Moving. Staring at the ground. Trampling her mother's flowers. Yellow tape fenced off the yard.

"Marybeth?" The call was soft. Faraway. Familiar. Important.

"Yeah?"

"Come back to me."

Yeah. She wanted to. And felt the chill on her skin. A cool night breeze. Not sweat on too hot flesh.

Sand squished beneath her boots. Making her unsteady. Waves lapped the shore. She was an adult. On Christmas Eve. With a friend...

A friend.

"Oh, God, Craig, it was horrible."

"Tell me about it."

As best she could she described what she'd seen coming home. "There was a group of them at the door. They tried to hold me back, but I pushed and squirmed and because there were so many no one got a good grip on me and I got through them."

"Them? Who?"

"Police, I guess. Paramedics, firefighters, maybe. I don't know. Everyone was in uniform, I know that.

"The front door led to a small foyer and then the living room. The place was full of people, most of them staring at whatever was on the floor by the couch. I went pretty much unnoticed in there. At least it seems that way.

"I pushed past someone, I remember the feel of hard metal against my arm, and then I saw what they were all looking at."

It was red. Everywhere. Pools of it. Moving. Slowly spreading across the carpet…

Blood.

Hands cradled her head. "Hey, Marybeth. Look at me."

The voice again. Telling her to open her eyes. She couldn't. Couldn't bear to see.

"Look at me. It's Craig. Only Craig."

Her lids flew open. And he was right. It was only Craig. Seen dimly through the blur of tears and darkness.

And this must be why the all-knowing, all-inclusive *they* had told her over and over that it was important that she talk about that afternoon. Tell people what she'd seen.

They'd said it would all come out at some point, in one way or another. And the longer she waited, the harder it would be.

A rational thought. Marybeth held on to that. And to the sight of Craig's eyes, filled with compassion and warmth and strength, gazing down at her.

"Her body was lying, folded backward on the floor beside the couch, her head bent, exposing her neck." Choking, Marybeth tried to draw in a deep breath. Managed a gasp. "He'd cut her throat."

CHAPTER FOURTEEN

FIGHTING WAVES of dizziness, Marybeth struggled to find that place outside herself. The omniscient one who oversaw, overheard, who narrated to her brain.

"It had just happened," she said, an eerie, just-before-a-tornado type of calm descending, her voice a monotone. "Her skin was still wet with blood."

"Can you sit?"

Noticing the boulder in front of them, Marybeth nodded. Sat.

"She'd been raped," she said, hardly feeling the cold, hard stone beneath her. "The skirt she'd had on when I left for school that morning…"

Oh, God, that skirt. She'd loved that skirt. Throat clogging, Marybeth couldn't stem the resurgence of agony. The tears.

"It…was…twisted…"

A minute passed. Then two. "Up around her waist."

She shuddered. Closed her eyes. Opened them to greet the beach, the night, the ocean. The beach.

"All those men, they were standing there—" She had to stop again, to get enough air to speak. "Standing there just looking at her while her private parts were all exposed…"

Shaking, trying desperately to find the calm, to accept that something so atrocious had happened to the woman she'd loved more than life, the woman who'd given her life, Marybeth fought dizziness.

"She was bleeding from down there, too…"

The cadence of waves never changed. Rush forward, slide back. Rush forward, slide back.

"They were taking samples…"

She knew that now. Back then the plastic gloves and baggies and tools had just been another source of confusion to her.

Back then, life had been in the process of ending.

"And then, when they shifted her…"

No. Don't move her!

"I could see her breasts…"

Tears streamed down her cheeks.

"He'd cut her bra and her nipples were…were…bruised and swollen and…"

Oh, Mama. What happened to you? How did this happen? How did you let this happen? Mama? Mama?

"Marybeth."

No one in the room knew her name.

"Marybeth." The voice spoke again. Softly. Firmly.

Help?

"Marybeth."

She was shaking so hard her teeth hurt. They were making noise. *Mama, can you hear me?*

"I couldn't let them see her like that…"

They had to stop. To leave her alone. Mama was hurt. Couldn't they see that?

Daddy? Where are you? Mama's hurt. Daddy?

Daddy wasn't there. Only she was. Running at those men, tearing through them, hitting out at them, throwing herself on top of her mother's naked body.

It was warm. But too still. Mama's arms didn't wrap around her. Her eyes didn't focus. They just stared, looking at nothing, all stupid and cold.

And she was wet. Marybeth could feel warm liquid seeping through her clothes and…

"Marybeth. Come back."

No. No, she couldn't. Couldn't go through it all again.

"Marybeth."

She heard her name. Again and again. She wanted to answer. But she had to cry. She had to just keep crying.

"Hey, come on."

Shaking too hard to move, she remained still. Wherever she was. Unmoving. Uncaring. Only aware of the agony.

Until arms were there. Around her.

Mama's arms? Recognizing her? Coming for her?

But no, of course not. Her mother was dead. Had been dead for fifteen and a half years. And she was on the beach. On a rock.

"You aren't alone this time." Ah, sweet words. Sweet, sweet words. Their meaning wasn't immediately clear. Wasn't real. But she recognized them. Liked them.

"Feel me, sweetie. Feel my arms wrapped around you. Holding you. You don't have to do it alone this time."

The gentle rocking motion was nice. Comforting. Made her want to sleep against the warm body beneath her cheek. A breathing body. Solid. Massive.

Clothed.

Craig.

"I'm so sorry, sweetie. So sorry. You should never have had to go through that. Any of it."

She was sorry, too. For so many things. The things she hadn't done, hadn't said. Hadn't been able to do. For her dad and the fact that she hadn't been enough to make him happy.

"I'm right here, Marybeth. You aren't alone."

Her body was warm. Secure. Safe.

She was taking comfort from another woman's husband. Lying against him. Soaking his shirt with her tears.

And when he shifted, moved, settling her weight more completely against him, her arms wrapped around him, clutching him to her with every ounce of energy she had left.

"BONNIE PULLED ME off her." The voice had a faraway sound. A little girl sound.

Craig had no idea how long he'd been holding Marybeth. And he didn't care. He'd sit forever if she needed him to.

Guilt, like a piece of sewage, weighed his heart. She'd suffered so much and there was so little he could do to help. Except keep the secret that would kill her if she were to know.

"She tried to get me to go to her house, but I wouldn't leave my mom. Or let anyone touch her. I'd scream anytime anyone got close."

"The scream from yesterday. From the nightmare."

"Probably. Yeah."

She was calmer now, her breathing only racked by the occasional hiccup as she leaned against him, her head tucked beneath his chin.

He wasn't surprised that she fit as though she'd been born to be there.

"They'd called my dad at work, but I didn't know that at the time. Once he got there, I must've calmed down some. I remember thinking that she'd be okay now that he was there to protect her."

Another bout of ragged breathing accompanied the words and he knew she was crying again. Softly this time. A grown woman mourning.

"He and Bonnie took me over to the Mathers's house. I can remember them, one on each side of me, holding me up. Someone packed some of my things. I have no idea who. I wasn't allowed back in the house for weeks. Not until the carpet had been replaced. And the furniture. And I'd had several sessions of counseling."

"I'm surprised your dad moved you back there at all."

"I wanted to go. Everything I had of my mom was in that house. And I couldn't bear to leave the Mathers. I came home to their house every day after school. Even when I was older and didn't stay long, I still stopped in to let her know I was home. And to play with Wendy."

He wanted to run his fingers through her hair as his mother used to do for him when he was sick. It had always, without fail, helped. But he dared not get that close. That intimate.

"I'm sorry," she said long seconds later, straightening. "I've completely fallen apart on you. Not much of a way for a hostess to behave. And on Christmas Eve, no less."

As if any of that pertained. Or mattered. "I'm guessing it's Christmas by now so you're off the hook on that one. And don't ever feel like you have to apologize to me. I'm honored that you shared all of this with me. I wouldn't change this night for anything. Unless I somehow had the power to go back and change what happened fifteen years ago."

Her grin barely soothed the anger-induced bile gnawing at his gut. Marybeth Lawson was one strong woman. A survivor. She was going to be okay.

And that didn't make any of what she'd suffered okay. There was no way to make something like that right.

"I'm not really sure what I do next," she said. "I'm incredibly embarrassed."

Sitting on his hands to keep them to himself, Craig shook his head, holding her gaze with his own. "Don't be. Please. Not ever."

"I'd rather you not have seen what a mess I really am. Up until now only Brutus knew."

"Absolutely nothing about you is a mess," he told her. "To

the contrary, I'm amazed at your strength. How you kept all of this inside all these years, I have no idea. And along with fighting those demons all on your own, you've managed to keep a soft heart, to continue to reach out to people, to care for them. You've built a successful business. A successful life."

Chin raised, she looked away, staring off into the black vastness where the ocean lay. Her hands, resting on the rock by her thighs, seemed to be holding her up.

"I'd like to believe you're right."

"Of course I'm right." The glance she gave him changed his course. "What makes you think I'm not?"

"A…friend…of mine challenged me recently. At the time I assured him, fully believing myself, that he was wrong. But I've been thinking about what he said ever since." Shrugging, she turned back to Craig. "Maybe he's right."

"Challenged you how?" What friend?

"That's probably not a conversation we need to be having."

"After all that we've been through tonight, I can't imagine anything we couldn't talk about."

She paused. Craig waited.

"The claim is that what happened to my mother stifled me. Sexually."

Oh. A little hot along the temple, Craig maintained his casual facade with difficulty.

"Are you stifled?"

"Yesterday I had a sixteen-year-old kid who I practically raised coming to me pregnant and needing my help and I, the old wise one, haven't ever even had sex."

He'd wanted to know. Needed to know. And knew she'd just given him a piece of information he should never have had.

Marybeth Lawson—his angel on earth, a mate of the souls—was as sweet and untouched as she looked. God help him.

"You want to amend that thought about me not being messed up?"

The derision in her voice tore at him.

"Absolutely not." But… "Do you consciously stay away from associations with men because of what happened?"

"I don't think so." She paused. "Maybe."

"Did they ever catch the guy?" The question stuck in his throat.

"Yeah. That same day. Mom had somehow pushed the button for the emergency number programmed on her phone and someone saw him running then get in a car a few streets over. He got away but it only took a few hours for them to trace him. The trial was short. He was sentenced to life without parole, but I didn't find that out until years later. I've always hoped he was killed in prison. I've heard rapists don't fare well there."

Depended on the rapist, Craig supposed. Or cruel twists of fate. None of that mattered right now. She did. And getting her healthy. Keeping her happy.

"Did you rest easier knowing he was off the streets?"

"Maybe. I suppose. I don't think I realized the full ramifications of what he'd done to her until later. Mostly what I remember then is hating him for hurting her. And missing her so much I thought I'd die."

His own breathing was a bit difficult at that point as he struggled for composure, picturing the sweet girl she'd once been, with a vital part of her ripped away in a tragedy that she could never have hoped to understand.

And could never forgive.

He had to help her. The conviction was so strong Craig couldn't question it. At all. He was the one she'd been able to talk to. There was no mistake in that. This job was his.

Dear God, he silently prayed to the being he'd pretty much cut out of his life too many years ago to count. *Guide me here.*

Show me the way. This is a treacherous road I walk, a tight-rope without a safety net. Use me to her good. Only to her good.

"Well, obviously, judging by your reaction to my unexpected entrance yesterday, you still carry around some of the fright." He chose his words carefully, listening for inner direction.

"Obviously." Her tone was dry.

"So why do you choose to live alone?"

"I'm not alone. I have Brutus. And beyond that, I'm not going to let the fiend rule my life. Ruin my life. I'm going to live as though I'm not afraid."

And maybe, if she lived like that, someday she wouldn't be? The plan, while not bad, left a lot to be desired in Craig's opinion.

Not that he had any right to one. "So do you think that what happened to your mother has rendered you unable to feel sexual attraction?" he asked, knowing that only with the grace of a power stronger than himself could he get through this as he intended. Knowing, too, that he couldn't leave her where she was, frozen in between the child she'd been and the woman she was to become. "Does it make you fear the act? Or men?" And, with their earlier conversation still in his mind, had to amend that statement to, "Beyond attraction, I mean."

As the silence drew out, he kept a firm hold on his mind.

"I've suspected, until recently, that I was incapable of being turned on."

He remained mostly impassive to the words. Patiently waiting for whatever else she might need to add.

"I don't know that it stems from an aversion to men. Or to sex. I've just thought that I'm too closed off from intense emotion to experience anything as consuming as sexual desire."

But could any young girl, after having seen her mother as she had, with the nudity, the blood, have intimate involvement without a flashback to that horrifying vision? And lose all sense of excitement in the process.

Except, of course, how would she know if she'd never gotten far enough to find out?

"You said until recently."

She turned then, her eyes glistening in the moonlight as she looked at him.

"Until you."

And that's when Craig knew that he'd just fallen off his precipice.

CHAPTER FIFTEEN

WORN OUT far beyond physical exhaustion, Marybeth traversed the sand beside Craig as they made their way to the car parked alongside the curb at the edge of the grass.

"I wonder if this—whatever it is that I have for you—is because I know you're taken," she said aloud, mostly because she couldn't find the wherewithal, after spilling so much of her life all over him, to keep her thoughts captive.

"I was under the impression that the *mutual* attraction was evident from the first day I checked into the Orange Blossom."

"Well, it was, but—"

"You didn't know then that I was married. I'd taken off my ring, remember?"

Right.

"So you think I am capable of the same sexual feelings as anyone else, I just haven't met the right guy yet?"

His silence left room for a flood of awkwardness, and Marybeth realized how ridiculous this situation had become—how perverse. It was Christmas Eve—Christmas morning—and she was on the beach talking to a married guest about her ability to get turned on.

After having confessed that she had the hots for him.

Definitely something went horribly wrong here. And it was up to her to fix it.

"Obviously you're capable of initial desire." Craig's unexpected words interrupted her attempts to concoct a rectification plan. "Based on what you've said, that's a fact, not something open for debate."

He let that hang out there, between them, until she couldn't stand it. "Yes." It was all she said. Hopefully a period on the end of his sentence. An ending to the conversation.

"What we don't know is if that feeling will carry you through to more than initial attraction. Will you still be turned on when a man actually touches you?"

Who knew? Who cared? She couldn't think about that. Not here. In the dark. In a sleeping world. Alone with him.

Something melted in her private regions, leaving a pool of liquid heat in its wake.

The car was still a quarter of a mile away.

"It could be that some subconscious fear of men, an aversion to the sexual act, has stifled your natural drive to pursue an intimate relationship…"

He continued, his voice mingling with the night air, the soft sound of the waves, forcing her to continue on a path she knew better than to follow.

"Or it could be that you're perfectly capable, physically and emotionally, of experiencing the fullness of a sexual encounter, but have built so many walls around your heart that those other feelings don't have a chance to live and breathe."

Either way, she was ruled by fear. Which made her a coward.

Marybeth didn't feel like a coward.

"For someone like you, sex would be so much more than body parts…"

What did he mean, *someone like her?* Like something was wrong with her? That she was somehow lacking? She'd ask, except that she couldn't get enough air past the constriction in her throat.

Still, she had all the right body parts. Just like everyone else.

"Maybe your psyche has decided you've been hurt enough and refuses to allow you to take the emotional risk were you to become intimately involved."

Was the man never going to run out of his dime-store diagnoses?

"Have you ever had an orgasm?"

The toe of Marybeth's boot caught in the sand. She wished it was her head. Buried down there. Safe and unseeing. Unhearing. Unknowing.

"I told you I've never slept with a man." Her voice was stiff, forced, as she prayed for the walk to end.

And tried frantically to ignore the part of her that wanted the night to go on forever—a time out of time, life away from life—alone with the man who, in physical presence, not just letters, made her feel safe.

A man who helped her feel all kinds of things she'd never felt—and liked far too much.

"Which doesn't answer my question at all."

He wasn't going to be a gentleman. Wasn't going to let her off the hook.

"Your lack of manners is shocking." She sounded like a sixty-year-old virgin schoolmarm.

Truth be told, a good part of the time she felt like one.

"Nice try, but we passed the point of manners a long time ago. Mutually."

He had her there. But nowhere else. She was not going to answer him.

"Have you?"

She trudged on through the sand.

"It's nothing to be ashamed of one way or the other, hon." The softness in his voice brought tears back to the surface. Oh, God, she wasn't going to fall apart another time. Was she?

Would she ever be herself again? In control?

"If you haven't, it's understandable. The things you experienced, saw, were beyond horrific. It's a testimony to your inner strength that you've managed to open your heart to life and friendships, bringing happiness to others every day…."

She was strong. She knew that.

"And if you have…well…it might not be talked about as much, but women have needs, too, and sometimes the only or best answer is to take care of them yourself. It's natural. Healthy. And—"

"I don't know." As she blurted the words her only goal was to stop him. Shut him up. Before she threw herself at him and begged him to strip off her clothes and finish what his advent in her life had started.

So she could then hate herself for the rest of her life. But at least she'd know…

"You don't know what?"

"Whether I've…you know…or not." There'd been a time, after James had refused to meet her, when she'd touched herself a time or two. The experience had been empty. Left her completely flat and feeling more stupid than anything else.

He didn't move closer. Walk faster. Or slower. Hands in his pockets, he just continued on down the beach.

"Then I'm guessing you haven't," he told her as though they were discussing linen colors. "That's something pretty hard to miss."

"It…felt good." To be touched there.

"Ah, sweets, it feels far more than good. When it happens, you'll see what I mean. The sensation is otherworldly. You leave yourself and fly for a second or two. Or longer. If you're lucky."

She wanted to ask him if he was ever lucky.

"Maybe that's just for a guy."

"No." She sensed, more than saw, him shake his head. "You'll have to trust me on this one. Women fly, just like men.

But from what I've read, and been told, there are a lot of women who don't ever fully experience orgasm, mostly because it used to be such a taboo thing to talk about—and maybe even do. A lot of women didn't know it was even possible. Decades ago, nice women serviced their husbands, right? They bore children. They weren't taught that the act of conception could be heaven for them as well as for their husbands. And certainly, if they did know, it wasn't something women talked about. It wasn't something mothers taught their daughters."

She wouldn't know about what mothers taught their daughters about sex. She and her mom hadn't gotten that far.

"What prompted you to do so much research on the subject?"

"Not what, who," Craig said. "And I haven't done all that much research. My mother taught me very early on the responsibilities I had to my manhood, as she called it. She wasn't going to preach to me about who and when, but when the time came, I was to remember two things. First, I always protected myself and the woman I was with."

"Wear a condom?" She couldn't believe this conversation was feeling so right. Natural.

Or at least okay.

"Yeah."

"And second?"

"I was never to take my own pleasure until the woman I was with was pleased, as well. If I couldn't please her, if she couldn't reach that point, I wasn't to do so, either. I was to be man enough, responsible enough, to stop."

She had to ask. "Did you do as she said?"

"I remembered."

"But did you do the two things?"

"I've had sex without a condom."

He was married. That was understandable.

"And the other?"

"Always."

They'd reached the car. But climbing in hardly distracted Marybeth's jealousy at all.

GLAD TO HAVE DRIVING as a diversion, Craig started the car, put it in gear, maneuvered the couple of blocks to Marybeth's home, pulled into the driveway and over to the guest area. Parked.

All without speaking, looking at and most especially without touching the woman seated next to him.

He smelled her, though. The fresh, flowery scent he'd been associating with her for the past year. And in spite of his will to the contrary, he felt her. The warm energy that pulsed from her encapsulated him. Buffeted him. Drowned him.

And more than anything he'd ever wanted before in his life he wanted to be the one to show Marybeth Lawson what it felt like to experience the ecstasy of release. To bring her fully alive. To prove to her that she was normal, and healthy. That she could know the ultimate joy of sharing herself, connecting herself, with another human being.

That she didn't have to live her life alone and lonely.

He knew he had the ability to make it happen.

And there was Jenny.

And there was Craig. He loved Marybeth. There was no denying that anymore. Probably hadn't ever been the opportunity for denial.

He couldn't ever share her life.

"Well…good…night." She stood at the entryway to the parlor that led through to her apartment, facing him. About to leave him to traverse that big winding staircase alone.

"Or…rather, a very early good morning. I'll still be serving breakfast at eight if you're awake and want to come down." She'd donned her hostess cloak.

He knew what it covered.

"Marybeth." Her gaze met his as he stepped closer and the doubt he read in her eyes matched the thoughts flowing through his own mind. Yet they couldn't seem to mask the undeniable drive to know more. Feel more. Connect more.

The last thought he had as his hand slid around Marybeth's waist and he lowered his head, after the realization that his wife would be hurt, was that Jenny would understand.

MARYBETH WATCHED his head descend.

And still she wasn't prepared for the jolt that rent through her entire being as Craig's mouth touched her mouth. Lips covering lips. Perfectly joined.

He was warm. Solid. Soft and commanding at the same time. Taking. Giving. Demanding that she meet him all the way. He supped on her, and Marybeth joined in the unfamiliar dance, knowing exactly what to do though she'd never done anything like it before. Tutored by an instinct she hadn't known she possessed, she tasted Craig, gave to him, opened her mouth and licked him, accepting his tongue against hers, along hers.

"Mmm." She didn't recognize the sounds she was making, or the energy coursing through her. Nothing mattered but assuaging the fire down below. With him. Feeling him there. Only him. Making her complete.

When he pulled her more firmly against him, her breasts against his chest were pinpricks of sensation, of need and a pleasure-pain she didn't recognize at all. It took her a second to realize that the hard protrusion pushing against her pelvis was his penis. The awareness shook her briefly, as did the flood of wetness between her legs.

With a whimper, Marybeth pulled Craig's head more tightly against her mouth, as though, if he only opened wide enough, she could escape inside, to slide down the delicious heat and drown.

To be gone forever from all that there was to escape, all the pain inherent in living, and know only this. Forever and ever. World without end.

Then it ended.

Whether it was him, or her, Marybeth didn't know, but someone pulled away. Simultaneously they stepped back, breathing raggedly.

And Marybeth turned and ran for her door.

SHE'D LAID THE TABLE, complete with warming trays, serving dishes and one place setting, when Craig arrived in the dining room at five minutes before eight on Christmas morning.

Eyeing the one plate he knew he'd guessed right in coming down early. She wasn't joining him.

She moved with more speed than grace as she pushed through the door, muffin basket and pitcher of orange juice in her hands, jerking when she saw him there, but not pausing. With the ease of one who'd repeated the motions often, she laid the basket beside his plate, poured the juice, set the container on the table in front of him and was back at her door without ever looking at him.

"Can you hold on long enough for me to apologize?" His words stopped her, but she didn't turn around.

"Please."

"You have nothing to apologize for," she said to the door.

Her words were knives in his heart. "You came to me as a friend, offered me your trust and your most intimate secrets." He hadn't been to sleep. Couldn't sleep. "And I betrayed that trust by allowing my baser instincts to get the better of me."

"Cut the crap, McKellips. You didn't do it alone."

Not only were her walls in place, they'd been fortified—

with him firmly on the outside. He'd never hated himself more than he did in that moment. He'd failed her.

Maybe he should go. Get out of her life. Be done.

What had ever given him the idea he was the one to help her? That he could help her?

What made him think he had anything to offer this woman that would bring her anything but more pain?

Some feeling of connection? What was that but justification, rot gut for explaining away weakness?

"I offered you a safe place in which to hurt, and to heal. A place where you could say anything, knowing that whatever you revealed would be honored, protected. Any weakness you portrayed would not put you at risk. I had your back in that place. And when your guard was down, without any warning to you I stopped being your protector."

"You have a habit of doing that."

"What?"

She turned. "Being too hard on yourself." The pinched lines around her mouth softened, not quite into a smile, but close.

And he recognized the truth in what she'd said. He didn't just know her. She knew him, too.

"Like someone else I know?"

"Probably."

"I've got another five days here," he said, when he'd just been telling himself he had to leave immediately. "It's Christmas Day. And there's this friendship that I've kind of become dependent on hanging in the balance. Do you think we can call last night a low point of human weakness and put it behind us?"

When she licked her lips—when his body immediately responded—he wondered who he was kidding.

"I guess."

"I promise not to touch you again."

She nodded. "That's the only way—"

"I know." Jenny's approval or acceptance notwithstanding, Marybeth couldn't be involved with a married man. It would destroy her. He knew that.

And he couldn't be involved with her period. Ever.

CHAPTER SIXTEEN

Monday, December 31, 2007

Dear James

I'm sitting here with my glass of champagne following what has become my New Year's Eve tradition—
spending it with you.

In honor of our new relationship, I am starting out
this new year by telling you what I do for a living. I own
a bed-and-breakfast, James, can you believe it? It was
willed to me by an aunt I hardly knew and…

Two pages later, pages filled with descriptions of the old
house she loved, Marybeth stopped to refill the glass. She had
an hour until the clock struck midnight and she'd be facing
another year of her life alone.

She stared at the dove on the shelf above the desk. A metal
sculpture designed specifically for her by the artist himself.

Craig's gift to her this Christmas.

Brutus glanced up at her without lifting his head. He was
depressed tonight. Missing Craig, she knew.

So…I have a holiday visitor. Or at least, I have had
for the past two years. He left this morning. New guests
arrive tomorrow night and I'll be full for the rest of the
month as people come to us to get out of the cold.

Stopping again, she took a sip. Read what she'd written. Thought of what she wasn't saying.

Odd, now that she'd convinced James to open up their relationship, to make their conversation more personal, she'd, for the first time, experienced something she didn't feel right sharing with him.

She had a holiday guest.

And a friend.

A man who, true to his word, had not touched her again once during their remaining time together. They'd rented bikes one day, rode for hours. They'd shopped. Taken a day to visit a little Swedish village about an hour's drive up the coast. They'd visited with the Mathers once. Briefly.

And he'd never laid a finger on her. Not even when he'd said goodbye.

She refused to be disappointed that the farewell kiss she'd been anticipating all week hadn't come to fruition. Craig was a real friend, saving her from herself.

> And now for some bigger news. Remember little Wendy Mather? We've stayed in touch all these years— her parents are still my closest friends—and two days before Christmas she came to tell me she's pregnant.

She filled him in on all the details.

> It looks like I might get custody of the baby until Wendy's through high school at least—maybe longer. At first, I offered because the solution seemed perfect for them and because I owe them so much.

But over the past week, the idea has taken on a life of its own inside me. I thought I wasn't ready for a family, that I had to get my business more firmly established, that I had to give it all my energy. But as I've been contemplating changes that will be necessary if the Mathers decide to take me up on my offer, I find that all can happen with very little damage to my daily routine.

I find, too, that I want this baby. More and more every day. I wake up thinking about waking up with it. I go to sleep thinking about it sleeping in its crib in the empty bedroom next to mine. I even took it shopping with me—figuratively, of course—this evening.

Thoughts of the baby had carried her through the near panic and despair of Craig's departure without a tear.

The clock is striking midnight, James. I'm toasting my glass to you, to fifteen and a half years of an incredible friendship, and to the different and expanding us that this new year brings.

Love,
Candy

Saturday, January 5, 2008

Dear Candy,

Forgive me if I seem bossy, or come on too strong. You're the strongest, most intelligent woman I've ever known. But after fifteen and a half years of committing myself to watching out for you, I can't stop.

Each letter you write to me I grow more and more concerned about you. More worried. We made it through a hellacious childhood, held each other's hands, were there for each other, and each time one of us faltered, the other was there to hold on, to pull us out of the mire.

We made it out so that we could live, my sweet friend. So that we could have in adulthood, that which was robbed from us in childhood. Love. Family. Belonging. The American dream. Right?

And barring all of that, we made it through with some hope that we'd someday find happiness. I know you wanted that, Candy. I was just rereading some of your letters and you told me so often enough. You just had to hang on, you said, happiness would come. Joy was your goal.

So tell me, my friend, what joy is there in living alone, in spending your days creating magic moments for others in lieu of having them yourself? I'm very proud of you—and gratified to know—that you've found a livelihood you love and are good at. One that is successful and provides security for you. One that allows you to tend to your friends at the nursing home and to use your culinary talents.

It truly settled my heart to read so much about that part of your life. Your satisfaction came through loud and clear and so many people never find that in a lifetime of searching.

But work is not the most important thing in life, sweetie. You know that. Remember your dad? You told me about how much you worried about his escape into work, as though the real him died with your mother and only the body was left.

So now I know that not only are you alone—with no prospects on the horizon for sharing your life—but then you tell me that you're going to step in and raise a baby for someone else? A baby that will be taken from you?

When are you going to stop subjugating your life to

everyone else? When are you going to stop facilitating for those around you and start living?

We saved you, Marybeth Lawson. I can't sit back and have you live life dead. (Your words in describing your dad.) I can't support this choice of yours. Not unless you are adopting the baby and he or she will be yours.

Wendy was your surrogate child at a time when you were too young to be a mother. You aren't too young anymore. Your needs and abilities and instincts are completely different—matured. If you think for one second you'll be able to mother this child from birth, then give it away two or four or six years later, you far underestimate your need to receive love as well as to give it. You are not protecting your heart on this one, my friend.

It is my job, at a time like this, to protect it for you.

I beg you. Please do not agree to take Wendy's baby with a condition that you will give it back.

Please.

You do that, and you risk losing any semblance of emotional well-being when the time comes to deliver.

Don't sell your heart short, Candy. It deserves to have its own people to love. You do not have to settle only for being a surrogate, a facilitator to the love of others.

I'd apologize for being harsh, but in all honesty I cannot do so. I am not sorry. I only hope and pray that my words still have the ability to reach your heart.

This is a new year, as you say. A new us. You wanted to enter this personal realm.

I couldn't worry about what I didn't know. Now I know. And I worry.

You are a part of my heart.

Yours always,

James

He'd called her Marybeth. For the first time in nearly fifteen years. Things were changing. Life was changing. And Marybeth had no idea what to do with any of it.

CHAPTER SEVENTEEN

Thursday, June, 12, 2008

Dear James

Okay, so during the six months of our new year, new relationship, you've revealed that you work in your garage every chance you get, that you're married, and that you don't have any children, that your wife doesn't want any.

Do you want any?

What do you do in your garage?

And what do you do for a living, when you're not in your spare time??? Are you using your Mechanical Engineering degree?

Yes, I've had a few guests that I didn't care for, but none that have given me any real trouble. You don't seem to see much of that in this business. At least not among the innkeepers I know. Yes, there are many of us in Santa Barbara, and yes, for the most part we hang together, sharing stories and warnings and chores and cleaning people when necessary.

And no, I don't think it's ever possible to say I love you too much, as long as the words are true. I think the statement is used too often in today's world to express fondness, or caring, instead of an expression of the deeper, more committed emotion. And that's when it becomes confusing—its message weakened. You know I believe love is an action, not a word and shouldn't be expressed unless one can act upon it. Meaning, one's heart reaches out to another's to the point of feeling their pain, their frustration, and needing to relieve it whenever possible.

I'm not speaking romantically here, but that comes to pass, as well.

And in that vein, I have news. I am fully engaged in the act of love. It's official. I'm going to be taking custody of Wendy's baby—it's a girl!—upon her birth until Wendy is out of school, be it high school or college. She will have full visiting rights, as will her parents, of course. But I will be the baby's sole guardian.

The Mathers have set up a trust account in my name and will be depositing money each month, but this is not part of the legal paperwork. And yes, dear James, I realize this means that at any time I could become financially responsible for this baby, but I don't care. I can swing it! I want to swing it.

I already hear your voice in my head, my friend. I haven't forgotten your letter of six months ago. I gave much thought to your concerns regarding this decision of mine, and I truly think that, in this case, I know better. I'm fully prepared for the hard times ahead. I believe the chance to help the people who've loved me unconditionally most of my life is worth the eventual sacrifice. When I do sign the baby over to Wendy, I will receive full parental visiting rights—I just won't be the custodial parent. That is all being written up as part of the court document that is going to make all of this official. As with general visitation, Wendy won't be able to take the baby out of state without my cooperation.

And to assure you that your words are heartfelt and valuable to me—I've been on several dates in the past few months. Not with the same guy but at least I'm accepting the invitations, opening up to possibilities. It's kind of funny, a little bit gratifying, and somewhat embarrassing to note that once word got out around town that I was going out, I've been receiving at least one call a week. But don't worry, it definitely won't go to my head. There aren't that many available women my age in Santa Barbara!

So far, there's not one guy who stands out above the rest, but I'm having a good time. And finding out some things about myself. For instance, I know now that I definitely do not like dating a man with a mustache. The good-night kiss was prickly. (Just kidding. I said that to mess with you.)

Seriously, I think I'm probably going through a belated high school maturation process where men are concerned. Most girls date in high school and find out what they do and don't like, want, enjoy, in the opposite sex.

So far, I haven't learned anything I didn't know, but we'll see.

I am determined to do this—for both of us. You made good points and I will do whatever it takes to live a healthy, joyful life. You know that.

And I have a question for you... Do you think joking can go too far? Or, if all parties understand that it's joking and someone's feelings still get hurt, is that someone being too sensitive? A debate I had this week with one of the more interesting dates.

At least he challenges my thinking!

Okay, I'm off. There's much to do around here to prepare for the baby that's due to arrive next month! I've got everything I need. Just decided, at the last minute, to paint the spare bedroom nursery. And, as always, I have a completely booked house from now until September.

I wish you were here. I wish so badly you could meet this new little one. We're calling her Kristy— after my mom.

Love always,
Candy

Sunday, June, 15, 2008

"YOU DON'T HAVE TO do this." Hands wringing, Marybeth watched as Craig filled a pallet with colors from the little cans of satin finish wall paint they'd purchased the day before on his lunch hour. She'd been fretting ever since.

As Brutus was now, locked in the kitchen so he didn't trudge into a bucket of paint. Or get high from the fumes.

"I feel like I'm taking horrible advantage of you. You've been crazy busy for three days and need to rest, not come here and work."

Three days that, other than lunch at the fair and breakfast in the company of others, and a quick trip to the store in separate cars, they'd hardly seen each other. She was busier than ever before. And so was he.

He was keeping his distance. She was letting him.

"You didn't ask, I offered," he said, squatting on the floor over the pallet as he glanced at her over the top of the can in his hand. "I want to do this."

Even the cheap jeans and white T-shirt he'd picked up the day before specifically for this occasion looked like a million dollars on him.

"I can't imagine why." She glanced away. "You told me once that you don't even like to paint."

"I don't like to work with canvas," he corrected. "And the answer is simple. I want to do it because it gives me an excuse to spend time with you while at the same time keeping us busy enough to avoid dangerous territory."

So he'd noticed it, too? The silent emotional explosion that had happened the second he'd walked in her door three days ago? The way he'd been acting, she'd thought she'd been the only one to have been affected by the blast.

"Now, can you please hand me that brush?" He'd stood, was climbing on the stepstool he'd set up in front of the rainbow flower garden mural he'd started the night before and just finished drawing.

She handed the brush. And another. She rinsed. Mixed. Cleaned. Gave opinions, and painted where she could.

"This is especially sweet of you, considering that you don't approve of my decision to take Kristy."

"It's not my decision to make."

"I know."

"And I have nothing against Kristy, though I'm not sure this is fair to her, either, depending on how long you have her. It's you I'm most concerned about. Look at you. You're head over heels in love already and you haven't given one thing to the kid yet. What are you going to be like after investing two or more years of your life, your heart and soul, with her?"

"You sound just like—" Marybeth broke off. She never mentioned James to anyone other than Bonnie who knew about him from the past.

Her father had known that she'd had a pen pal, but they'd never spoken of him. No one knew how much she relied on her paper friend. For several reasons. But one very good one. They'd all tell her the dependency wasn't healthy. That it was keeping her from living a normal life—from really living, as James had said.

She didn't want to hear it.

Craig wasn't painting. He was looking at her. "Sound like who?" His gaze was intent.

"Nothing. No one. Just someone who, when they heard what I was doing, gave a lot of the same reasons you do as to why it wasn't a good idea."

When he turned back to the wall, she relaxed. "Must be someone close to you, to give such a personal opinion."

Did that mean he considered himself close to her?

"He is."

"He?" The brush dipped into paint and delicately filled small spaces.

"Yeah."

"Does he have a name?"

Stifling her first instinct to say no, Marybeth considered the ramifications of telling this…man…this guest…this friend who she saw only twice a year and never heard from in between, the name of her most trusted friend.

A name that wasn't even real.

"James."

His brush was in the color. And back on the wall. "Tell me about him."

Oddly enough, she wanted to. God, how she wanted to.

Because a part of her—a growing part of her—feared that the critics in her head were right. Her dependency on James could be robbing her of the ability to love in real life.

What man could ever live up to him? Except perhaps the one who'd left the delicate rainbow edges unfinished and moved on to much wider flower petals.

And how real life was Craig? Married and, even if he weren't, not interested in a long-term, permanent relationship with her. Seeing him twice a year wasn't much different from seeing James only in letters.

And maybe exactly what James had predicted was true. Did she really have an inability to love a man except from afar?

"James is a guy I write to."

"Where'd you meet him?"

"I never have." And that easily, after sixteen years of keeping him hidden, Marybeth fell into a half hour dissertation starting with when she met James—something that wasn't so hard to introduce after her Christmas revelations to this biannual soul mate of hers—and ending with the fact that they still wrote to each other every single week.

Craig finished six flowers, their stems and part of a colorful path as he listened.

"Obviously he means a lot to you," was the first thing he said when she fell silent.

"I don't know what I'd do without him."

"Oh." He shot her a glance, then turned back to his road. "You're much stronger than you give yourself credit for. If you had to, you'd do just fine without him. I mean, what is he, really, but a piece of paper?"

Exactly what she'd told herself a thousand times. So why did it make her so mad, so defensive to hear the words said aloud?

"You have no idea what you're talking about," she said now, wishing, already that she'd kept her secret friend to herself. No one was going to get it. No one.

But that didn't make it wrong. Or unhealthy.

No one could understand.

Not unless they'd walked in her and James's shoes all these years.

"James is a man, Craig, with thoughts and feelings, opinions and a heart. No different from you. Just because I haven't physically met him doesn't mean that he doesn't exist. His soul is every bit as alive, valid, as yours is."

He painted on, apparently willing to finish the job he'd started even if she'd offended him.

For the moment, she didn't care if she had.

"He was a boy of thirteen when he first took me on," she said, her voice shaking. "Not once, in all these years has he left me hanging—forgotten me or refused to write. Not once has he belittled me, or made me feel insignificant."

"It's easy to be perfect when it's only once a week in a medium where you get do-overs before you send."

"He's not perfect," she said. "Not by a long shot. Sometimes he plain pisses me off. And before you jump to another wrong conclusion, he doesn't always agree with me, either.

"Kristy's a case in point. He adamantly states his belief that I'm making a mistake. He's resorted to begging me to reconsider.

"And when I don't," she continued, handing Craig the can of orange paint when she saw that his pallet supply was nothing but smears on plastic, "he won't desert me. If what he predicts comes to pass, he'll still be there, supporting me as I hurt my way through."

"Again," Craig said, handing back the can, "it's easy to be patient, to continue to be there when you never really have to be there at all."

"Of course it is. You think I don't know that the parameters of the relationship allow him to be more than anyone else ever could be?"

"I wondered."

"You think I don't know that his existence makes it hard for anyone else to live up to him, to make me feel as though I can rely on them every bit as much?"

He turned to look at her, piercing her with his gaze. "Do you know that?"

"Yeah. But that works both ways, you know. James will never be the one I call in a crisis. How could he be? Letters take days. And even if I reached him by phone, it's not as though he could come to me. One of our understandings is that we can't meet.

"He'll never be the one I turn to when I need a hug. Or the one I shop for, cook for, clean for. He'll never be the one I make love with. He'll never be anyone I do anything for, except write a weekly letter."

"So how can you say that losing him would be so catastrophic?"

"Because James is like the best part of me." As she said the words aloud, things finally started to make sense to her. "He sees the best me and shows her to me on a regular basis. He challenges her. He tells her when he thinks she's wrong. But he always sees her. Always believes in her. And because he's been so faithful in showing her to me, I see her, too."

She paused as she started to choke up. "Look at me, Craig. I've lived through hell, grown up without the usual love and support a kid needs, and I'm a relatively well-adjusted, happy, successful person. And it's not because of any counseling I went to after my mother was murdered. It's because I know me. I'm in touch with me.

"James gives me that. I have the courage to be wrong, because I know that, no matter what, I'm good enough. How many people in this world have that?"

He was sitting on the stepstool, his gaze intent as he watched her. "Not many, I'd guess."

"There's something else, too."

"What's that?"

"I've never felt unloved," she said. "I've never felt like I don't have value. James's faithful communication, through so many years and distractions and changes, shows me how much I mean to him. Whenever I'm feeling the most down, I think of him and I know, without a doubt, that I am loved."

CHAPTER EIGHTEEN

THE MURAL WAS DONE. Half an hour past midnight—much later than he'd hoped—but judging by the smile on Marybeth's face, he'd more than met her expectations.

And in the morning, right after breakfast, he'd be leaving to head back to Colorado. And Jenny.

"I think that I pushed too hard," she'd said before he left, speaking of their marriage. "Rather than listening to you when you tried to tell me that you couldn't give me all of you, I promised you that you wouldn't make me lonely because I lived in the moment and my moments with you were happy. And, I think, for the first time, in spite of your fears that you couldn't fully engage, you actually believed that you might not have to live your life lonely, either."

In the morning, Craig would be saying goodbye to Marybeth again, for another six months.

"Have the courage to live outside your art, Craig," Jenny had said in that conversation that had stripped him of confidence. "Really live. I don't know all of what happened to you when you were a kid, only bits and pieces your mother told me, but somehow this woman has the ability to unlock whatever got trapped inside you."

This woman. Marybeth Lawson.

If only Jenny knew.

"You've missed your libations every night this time

around," Marybeth said now as they turned off the lights in the spare room and walked toward the kitchen and the door leading him to the guest portion of the house. "Would you like a glass of wine now? A nightcap before you go up?"

He'd love to have the night continue forever, but Jenny's words played in his mind, as they'd been doing pretty much nonstop since he'd left home. "She is your freedom from the demons that haunt you."

"You have to be up in less than six hours," he said now.

"I'm fine on four hours of sleep," she said. "I can always nap after breakfast. Besides, I figure I need to get used to surviving on less sleep. I'm going to be doing feedings every two hours in a matter of weeks."

The baby. Kristy. He'd just spent hours painting her nursery.

At least he'd been able to be a small part of this momentous time in Marybeth's life. And maybe she'd think of him, sometimes, when she was in the nursery he'd painted, rocking the baby during those middle of the night feedings.

And in the morning. And after her nap. And…

"So, would you like a drink or not?"

God, he was tired. And dreading tomorrow, responding to Jenny's observation: "Maybe I don't want to be what you settle for because you can't have what you really need."

"Yes. If you'll join me." How was he ever going to say goodbye to Marybeth?

In light of the fact that the inn was filled with guests she didn't want to disturb at this late hour, Marybeth suggested that they sit at the table in her kitchen. And fifteen minutes later, he knew that any thoughts he might have entertained about cutting her out of his life—or, more properly stated, getting out of hers—were only that: thoughts. Just as he could never have a real life with this woman, he could never desert her, either.

Which meant he was going to have to get used to telling her goodbye. And letting go.

"I know it's none of my business, but, well, maybe it is, considering our previous conversations…"

"And considering the fact that you're sitting in my kitchen at almost one o'clock in the morning drinking wine?"

God, the woman did things to him.

"Okay, that, too," he said with a smile, trying not to relax too much. He was not going to let things get out of hand. So much was at stake. Lives and hearts—which were far more important than any physical satisfaction anywhere.

But she was beautiful beyond the expected. The T-shirt dress she wore hugged her in all the places Craig wanted to, tightening across her as she moved. He could see the lace of her bra through it. And the thin strap across her back. One snap of his fingers and he could have it undone….

"Um, what were you going to say?" Her lips had a slight tremor as she attempted a smile, but her eyes gave her away. She knew where he'd been looking. And had an idea of what he'd been thinking, too, judging by the hard buds her nipples had become.

"I was going to say…" he started, struggling to pull his thoughts back. "I have another big concern about this baby thing."

"Besides my eventual heartache and the baby's parental confusion if I keep her too long? And the long hours, and possible financial burden? And being a single parent?"

He tried to look chagrined, but had a pretty good idea he failed. He stood behind every single objection.

"Yes, in addition to all that."

"So lay it on me."

He'd like to lay on her.

Growing desperate, Craig attempted to distract himself

with her kitchen, noting its pristine shape, the chrome every-thing, that rack with pans hanging from the ceiling. He was going to have to see about having a treated wood cooking island like hers installed at home.

Home. Colorado. His real life.

"You had a huge breakthrough over Christmas," he said, focused again as he met her gaze. "Talking about your mom, recognizing that the past was holding you hostage from being fully alive. From what you've said over lunch these past few days, you've actually enjoyed dating. You've got prospects practically knocking your door down. You add a baby to that mix and I'm guessing most of those men will fade away."

"I know that."

"So, what, you're using Kristy as another excuse to keep yourself at arm's length from any personal intimacy?"

"No. I'm not using her at all. But if having her here helps weed out the players, then so be it. At least this way I'll know. If a guy is willing to be a part of my life with a baby in tow, he's got some depth to him."

He couldn't argue with that. He tried to work something up, though.

"How's Jenny?"

Did she know? Had she figured him out, too? "Fine. Why?"

"You haven't mentioned her once since you've been here."

"We've hardly had a chance to talk this time around." The wine was good. A bottle of it, consumed all at once, would have been better.

"So, talk. How are things?"

Guys didn't share troubles. Or, if they did, it was only when seeking an immediate solution—something that was largely out of his hands on this one. He couldn't make Jenny want him.

Couldn't make her settle for less. He didn't want her to settle for less.

He couldn't give her more.

The violet depths of Marybeth's eyes drew him in. "We're going through a trial separation." The words sounded so much worse aloud. And they'd been pretty horrible in the silence of his mind.

"What? What happened? It wasn't…it's not because… We didn't do anything—"

"I know. It's not you. Or…us." That one word sent another cascade of inexplicable emotion swirling through him. Confusing him.

"We're still living together, just not as husband and wife for a bit."

It hadn't been any clearer to him when Jenny said it. "I'm not asking for a divorce, Craig. At least not yet. I'm not sure I want one. Or could even bear to give you up. All I know is that things are changing and we're going to have to change with them. We need some time to figure out whether we make those changes together or apart. I think, when we started out, we were perfect for each other, just what each other needed. But lately, since you've been going to Santa Barbara, I've been wondering if maybe we've outgrown each other. Maybe what was once so good is now holding us back from more."

"I don't understand," Marybeth said.

That made two of them.

"She's not sure she loves me anymore."

"How could she not love you?"

Craig didn't know what moved him more, the instantaneous defense, or the blush that crept up Marybeth's cheeks as her words rang out.

"Easy," he told her, pushing through the moment. "I haven't given her much to love."

"You're you, Craig. It's not a matter of doing, or being enough. It's just—"

He shook his head, cutting her off. "No, in this case, she'd be right. Jenny and I have been married for almost eight years and she doesn't even know that I have a father in prison. Or that, when he writes to me every month, to a post office box that was established ten years ago, I don't so much as open the envelopes."

"You have a father in prison?"

He nodded. And couldn't tell her more. He'd already said too much.

"Do you send the letters back?"

"No. I toss them."

"But you keep the post office box."

"He knows my name. He could find me."

"And then the letters would come to your home."

"Right."

"Don't you think, maybe, you ought to read at least one of them? I mean, whatever he did, maybe he's incredibly sorry, maybe he's spending the rest of his life atoning for it. Maybe he can explain. And no matter what, God offers even the worst sinner complete absolution and forgiveness. Right?"

"I'm not going to read them."

Marybeth didn't argue aloud, but her eyes said so much. "So Jenny doesn't know about him—that certainly doesn't make you a bad husband."

Funny how Jenny had said almost the same thing. "You couldn't be a bad guy if you tried, Craig McKellips. That's part of the reason I'm addicted to you. You are loyal and kind. I've never met anyone so aware of his own responsibilities to others. You make a person feel completely, elementally safe with you."

Brutus stood, nudged Craig's hand, bringing him back once again from the deadening conversation. "She doesn't know I like dogs," he told Marybeth. "Or that I actually like to cook."

And if he put an island in their kitchen, she'd probably not notice that.

"She doesn't know that the beach speaks to me, that I find peace and belonging there. Or that I want children. Or that I think giving away a baby is one of the hardest things anyone could ever do.

"She has no idea how much I miss my mother."

Words continued to rush to the surface; the deeper he reached the more he found.

"If you told her that I believe in a spiritual, soul-mate connection between two people, she'd be stunned."

"So tell her."

A solution he'd considered. Was still considering.

"The one thing she does know is how to find me in my work," he said, his thumb rubbing back and forth against the stem of his wineglass. "She's always been good at that."

"So you have a connection. You might simply need to expand on it."

If she wanted to. If he did.

If there was enough feeling there to sustain them.

"Do you want the marriage to work?"

"Of course." Pausing, Craig met Brutus's laconic stare. "The thought of losing Jenny has me in knots."

"That's your answer then, isn't it?"

Was it? He didn't know. And didn't know why he didn't know.

"Do you believe there really is someone for everyone?" He asked one of the questions he'd been mulling over fruitlessly. "Someone who is out there waiting to be found?"

"Don't you?"

"I didn't used to."

She licked her lips. "And now?"

"Now, I think there might be. For most people."

"Said like a true cynic on the verge of reform." The soft smile on her lips made the words almost an endearment.

"Tell me something," she said next. "Do you feel safe or threatened at the thought of baring your soul to your wife?"

Holding back the response that sprang to his lips—that he'd never do it—Craig considered what she was really asking, the ramifications.

Did he trust Jenny with his heart?

"I don't know," he finally offered, draining his glass. The reply wasn't prevarication. It wasn't diversion or avoidance or a coward's way out.

It was the absolute truth.

Sunday, June 22, 2008

My dearest Candy,

I have much to tell you, but first, in response to your debate with the jokester. I think it all depends on the situation and how well you know the people. It depends on the audience and how you define a joke. On one end, it can be a form of abuse, where the jokester says hateful things and doesn't take responsibility for them by way of brushing them off as jokes. He gets to say whatever mean things he wants without being accountable. He's just a funny guy, right?

On the other hand, at a comedy club, you go there knowing that the person on stage is joking, entertaining and that you or something important to you could be the butt of a joke. So in that situation, if you get your feelings hurt, it's more on you because you chose to be there knowing the circumstances.

If you're with someone who jokes a lot, and he or she is a nice person and you know they wouldn't hurt you, and you take offense at the joke, that probably isn't fair to that person, either. It's understood, in that kind of situation that the person is free—allowed—to be him or herself and let it fly and then when offense is taken, the joker feels horrible as no harm was ever intended. Right?

With a smile on her face, Marybeth walked to the back of her yard, entering the white trellised gazebo area that, at the moment, was unoccupied. Her guests were all out for the day and she was enjoying this moment with James.

His analyzing of joking, so James-like, brought her back to the sense of self she needed. This was normal. Her life. He threw himself into any topic. And could break it down to manageable levels.

He'd taught her to do the same.

She'd lost sight of that under all of the baby clothes and diapers and formula stacked up in the nursery. The baby was due any day now.

I wonder, do you mind if I tell my wife more about you than just the fact that we write? I won't share our letters. I will never, ever do that, you have my word. But I'm turning over a new leaf with her, trying, in light of our conversation about fully living, to be as brave as you are and open up to living fully. This means the tenure of my relationship with her has to change.

I will do nothing until I hear back from you. This is all still in the thinking stage anyway. But I cannot push you or expect you to take risks that I am refusing to take myself.

The letter continued, telling her about some remodeling he was doing, about a business trip from which he'd just returned, that he was taking up jogging. Marybeth hung on every word—mentally trying to escape from his request.

Life was changing so much. So fast.

She should never have told Craig about James. Especially not without talking to him first.

She didn't want him telling his wife about her.

There'd be judgments.

Other people in their precious space.

And now, Candy, I have a question for you. Is there a difference between the words, "I love you" and "love you"? Does one hold me apart from fully giving while the other sinks me right into the thick of promises? Or do they both say the same thing in different ways? When I say "I'll see you later," it's because I have plans to see that person in the near later. On the other hand, when I say "see ya" I'm really just saying goodbye to someone I have intentions of seeing again sometime in an indeterminate future.

I'm shaking my head as I reread this. Do you have any idea what people would say if they could see what I write here? I'm nuts. Analyzing life to death. Thinking too much. Creating drama.

Maybe.

But if so, I sure love doing it with you. I look forward to your answers every single week. And take them with me as I go about my days. You give life depth, my Candy. You make it far richer than I ever imagined possible.

I daresay our lives are far more layered and dimensional than most, based on our conversations here. I don't ever, ever want to lose that.

I promise you.

Forever,

James

CHAPTER NINETEEN

Monday, July 7, 2008.

Dear James

Do you have to be right so much of the time? Do you have to be right *this* time?

Precious little Kristy was born last night.

When a tear dripped from her chin to the stationery, Marybeth stopped. Grabbed a tissue. And went right back to writing.

Talking to James was the only thing she knew to do right now. The only way she knew to cope.

She's everything we knew she'd be. Tiny. Dark hair, though the doctor says she'll probably lose most of it. Blue eyes but that might change, too. You should see her tiny fingers and toes. She has the smallest nails I've ever seen. She weighed in at a healthy seven pounds and is nineteen and a half inches long. Boy, does she have lungs!

And I don't get her, James. When the Mathers saw how much Wendy loved her baby, when they saw what the idea of losing her was doing to her, they realized that sometimes life matures people early and while that isn't the choice they'd have made for their daughter, she's a mother now. They can't change nature. They're going to keep the baby with them, help her all they can and she'll just have to have a different life than they all envisioned. She won't be able to be as active in school, or go away to college.

Wendy was so happy, James. Those other things were important to all of us. They weren't important to her at all.

At one point, Bonnie looked at me and said that I took over an entire house at twelve, I matured much too quickly, and yet look how I turned out. And she's right. We don't always get to choose our life circumstances. They aren't always going to be what we'd script. But what really matters is not so much the circumstances but what we do with them. Right?

Anyway, I'm bereft here in my apartment with baby things all around. I'll be taking them all over to the Mathers later today. But I can't take away the painted walls in the nursery.

Or the dreams in my heart.

I really wanted her, James.

Wendy cried when she looked at me. She feels terrible. But this isn't her fault. Giving me the baby wasn't her idea. She didn't want to do it from the first. It was the only way her parents would agree to forgoing a formal adoption.

No one thought taking the baby away from me later would be fair. I'm the one who insisted that was the way to go.

I guess God, fate, agreed with everyone else, huh? I really didn't see it clearly.

Damn. I hate that.

I'm so thankful you're there, James. While you could be jumping for joy right now at this news, because you were so worried and you got your way, I know better. You're crying for me, figuratively, aren't you, my friend? Right now you care more about the fact that I'm hurting than you do that you were right and I've been saved from a horrible mistake, don't you? It's like I can feel you there, suffering with me.

I guess you really can get to know someone well with only pen and paper correspondence.

I'm going to go for now. I need to reassure Brutus that the world isn't ending. And to get the baby things out of here so they aren't a constant reminder. But I will be taking you with me every moment of this day.

Kind of convenient that I can do that while you're still there taking care of your own business, huh?

I read something recently written by a female psychiatrist. She said that real love was when you could be apart with peace because you knew, no matter where your loved one was, they were always with you. It was as though she was looking in my heart and seeing you.

Love always,

Candy

P.S. Of course tell your wife about me.

Thursday, July 10, 2008

My dear, sweet Candy,

I am so sorry about little Kristy. I'm sorry that you're hurting. Your heart deserves happiness and I hope that it doesn't take long for this wound to heal. So many times over the years I've lain awake at night wishing I could do something to ease the burdens you've carried—and to guarantee you happy years ahead. And when I get frustrated at my own lack of ability to make things perfect for you, I pray as hard as I know how, to a God I'm not even sure I believe in. I'm praying now.

Remember how we talked about clichés being clichés because there's real truth in them and that is what guarantees them longevity of life? I'm about to prove the point.

Whenever a door closes, a window opens. Or another door does.

Please keep your eyes open so that you see that window. Or door. Something will come to you. Something that will bring you more than you ever envisioned with Kristy. I believe this with all of my being.

I must go as my wife and I are leaving for a weekend retreat in the Rocky Mountains, but your letter came this morning and I couldn't go without answering it. I will keep my phone with me at all times. You have my cell number. Please use it if you need me.

Right or wrong, kind to others or not, you are a part of me, Candy. A part that is more integral to me than anything else I've ever encountered in life. I've come to realize this over several months of personal introspection and searching. There is much that I do not know, many things for which I cannot find answers, but this I know. I cannot give you up. Ever.

You are the top of my pyramid.

Yours,

James

Sunday, December 7, 2008

Dear James,

I can't get your most recent letter out of my mind. How can you say, at twenty-nine, that you know for certain you'll never have children? I understand that your wife doesn't want kids. That you say you don't. But as we learned very early on in life, things change all the time. Who knows, ten years from now, what you will have experienced? And what choices you'll make because of them?

That you think you aren't father material is just plain nuts. You're patient, open-minded and have the insights of a saint. You see things, you know them, your understanding of people and situations, emotions and the world is unsurpassable. You can get through the muck to find the real problem, and make it seem simple. You don't get shaken easily. You care deeply. You are an excellent teacher. You know how to let others make their mistakes, then to be there for them to support them through the consequences without a single "I told you so." You'd be an incredible father.

That you think you know nothing about fathering because you grew up without your own father is unfathomable to me. While example is great, you don't need a father to be one. Fathering is instinctive.

Besides, you had your dad when you were young. You said so. Although, come to think of it, you've never told me how old you were when he split. Was it after the rape?

I can't believe we never talked about that. You never mentioned him and we always had so much to say and only a few pages to say it and I just followed your lead and let it go. I'm very sorry about that.

Especially now that I know his absence has left a crater-size mark on your heart. I feel like I let you down, my friend. I should have seen. Should have known.

Anyway, if you're really happy at the thought of a childless life, then so be it. If your heart aches at all at the thought, please don't close that door forever.

It makes me sad to think of you without kids.

And this brings me to my philosophical contribution

for the month. What do you think about the use of sperm donors? Is it right for a man to just give away his seed, thus giving away all responsibilities of fatherhood, and yet, contributing to the creation of a child that will now never know his biological father? Or, perhaps, any father.

Who is the father? The sperm? The heart that cares for the child? The man who knows him (or her)? Who raised him? What about the men who raise their children and suck as fathers? The ones who beat their kids? Or, in my mind just as bad, neglect them? Failing to have time for them. And what about the men who died young? Are they any less their children's father?

Why are some men responsible for the lives they create and others aren't? What defines fatherhood? A paper that is signed at a clinic? Or a name on a birth certificate? Is fatherhood a matter of legality? Or genes?

I've spent these months since I lost Kristy looking more deeply at life than ever before. I guess you could tell that, huh?

She's doing great, by the way. I had her over here yesterday for the afternoon. I keep her once or twice a week—usually when Bonnie has to take Bob to therapy. Their family has really pulled together with the advent of this little one. I think they made the right decision to keep her. No child has ever been more wrapped in love.

Randy is over there every day, too, and helps Bonnie with Bob as much as anything. Kristy adores him. He's a freshman at Santa Barbara City College, getting his general ed studies done before he transfers to Cal State. I think he and Wendy will marry before then. They haven't said, but my guess is they're planning on next summer, after she graduates from high school. She'll work and take care of Kristy while he finishes his last two years, and then, when he starts work, she can quit and go to school.

Not ideal, by the world's standards, but really, why not? Her favorite fun time growing up was playing house. More than anything she wants to be a wife and mother. A worthy goal, if you ask me. One of the most important.

I must go. Grace just arrived and we have a full turnover today with repeat guests so lots of special instructions.

I'm worried about you, my friend. These past few months you've seemed troubled. Your letters are shorter, your responses less confident.

Talk to me. Please.

Love always,

Candy

Thursday, December 11, 2008

Sweet Candy,

As always, it was so good to get your letter. You have an uncanny ability to know exactly when I most need to hear from you.

And, also as usual, your perception is more accurate than not. I have been troubled over the past couple of months…years. I don't know if it's that I'm turning thirty next year—fully into adulthood—or if it's losing my mom, but I have been instilled with an urgency to find whatever is missing from my life.

I continue to struggle to figure out what that something is. Do I have it here, right in front of me, but can't see it? Can't find it?

Am I trying too hard?

Or is this elusive something calling out to me to come find it?

As to your sperm question—I believe that sperm banks serve a purpose. As with most things, there are negatives, downsides, regarding the donation and use of sperm. I don't think children should be bought and sold, for instance, and sperm are there only for the creation of children, right? But overall, I think they serve a worthy purpose—allowing couples who might not be able to conceive in the normal way to have children that they will love and raise to make a positive impact on society and the world.

I think of how much my mother loved me, loved being a mother, and it bothers me to think of other women like her, not having that opportunity because of a function of biology.

On the other hand, I have mixed emotions about single women impregnating themselves without any intention of having a father figure, or other male influence in the child's life. Maybe because I grew up without a father, but I believe—especially for boys—that a father adds a vital ingredient to the mix of growing up.

With James's letter received two days ago written as clearly on her mind as it was on paper, Marybeth finished preparations for the morning's breakfast—a sausage casserole that had to refrigerate overnight—washed the dishes and told herself to go to bed.

Which she was doing, by way of standing in the archway between the kitchen and her sitting room. Watching her from his prone position in the hall leading to the bedrooms, Brutus grunted.

You're going to do it, aren't you? his big brown eyes seemed to say. There wasn't judgment there. At least not that she could see.

"What?" she asked the dog aloud. "I should clean off the top of the desk," she told him. "I finished all the Christmas cards last night. And we're booked solid through the twenty-third so I'm going to have to get all the Christmas baking and presents wrapped in between regular cooking and guests."

He didn't respond.

She'd be booked through New Year's except that, as always, she'd blocked the week of Christmas for her lone holiday visitor.

He'd made his reservation before leaving in June.

And she hadn't heard from him since.

Did that mean he'd patched things up with his wife?

Turning her back on her two-hundred-pound, furry conscience, Marybeth moved to the desk.

It was perfectly clean.

She'd known that, of course. After all, she'd been the one to clean it. But James's letter was there.

The desk was where she wrote her letters to James.

And that's when she knew she was going to ask him. The worst he could do was say no. She'd survived that before. She could do so again. And if she didn't ask him, she knew she'd regret it for the rest of her life.

Nothing, not even an outrageous question, would come between them or in any way affect their friendship. They were unconditional.

As long as they didn't meet.

Wednesday, December 17, 2008

Dear James,

I have decided to have a baby. There are several reputable sperm banks in the L.A. area and I've already met with a couple of them. The procedure is fully confidential, medically sound and relatively affordable. Pregnancy is not guaranteed, of course, how could it be? But there are packages that offer options for repeated attempts.

Part of my reason for choosing a sperm bank—beyond the obvious one of not wanting to sleep with a man I don't love—is so that the father can remain unknown to me. I won't have to deal with possible custody battles, or having a child split between homes.

I promise, my friend, that there will always be male influences in the child's life. Randy and Wendy and Bob and Bonnie all fully support my decision. Bob and Randy have already volunteered to be surrogate dad and granddad.

And I have my nursing home friends—many of whom are male and who will grandparent whether I ask them to or not.

There are men at church.

And I continue to date, though, as of yet, no one lights a spark.

I have fully considered all angles of this decision and realize that I am, in some ways, making my life more difficult than it need be by taking on the responsibility of being a single parent.

And yet, when weighed with the idea of life zooming by before I can find a man with whom I can fall in love, a man I truly would want to spend the rest of my life with, a man who could traditionally father my children, the difficulties seem minimal.

More catastrophic to me would be to miss the chance to be a mother.

I had the best of all examples.

I realize that I minimize my chances of having men showing interest in me when I come with a baby in tow, but as I said before, this added concern is really a blessing to me. I wouldn't want a man who was unwilling to love my child if he loved me. So this would really just serve to weed out the sure losers!

Now, dear friend, I have a question to ask you. Please read on only if you fully understand that a no answer is as favorable as a yes one would be. Either way, you are guiding my life in the direction it needs to go.

I want to know, my love, if you would be willing to donate the sperm for my baby. I've checked with the clinic and we could do this very simply. The specimen would be frozen and flown to the clinic of my choice in L.A.

I've thought of little but this since the idea first occurred to me last July. While we will never physically meet, what a perfect joining of you and I. A true blending of us, a culmination of our love—without the sex. The kind of love we share is so beyond sexual, so beyond this world. Can you imagine the child that would result from that?

Of course we would do all of the necessary legal paperwork, fully discharging you from any responsibility for the child. And, of course, your wife would have to be agreeable. I'd need that in writing from her.

The woman's lack of desire for children was partially what allowed Marybeth to even make this request. She would not take a child from its rightful mother.

And the woman was partially the reason she'd put off asking the question. What if James wanted to do this and she said no? He'd be forced to choose.

Which was why she wasn't going to go through with the procedure, no matter what James said, unless his wife was on board.

There was so much more she had to say—different ramifications and joys—resulting from her proposal. But she didn't want to sway him. Nor to think for him.

She'd had months to mull this over, to conjure up pros and cons and in betweens.

Putting pen to paper once more she wrote, simply,

I love you, my friend, and am filled with an elation beyond description at the thought of carrying your child within me.

At the same time, if it is not to be, I will be fully at peace with the knowledge that it wasn't meant to be. More than anything I do with my life, I need to support you. I mean that.

As always, I send you me,
Candy

CHAPTER TWENTY

Tuesday, December 23, 2008

CRAIG WAS LATE. Over an hour.

With snicker doodles—no longer warm from the oven—still undisturbed on the plate, just as she'd arranged them earlier, Marybeth took a deep breath.

"He's coming," she told the dog who was lying in front of the doorway, whether to greet their guest or because he was lazy, Marybeth hadn't decided.

She'd been telling her companion for more than a week about Craig's imminent biannual readvent into their lives.

Running upstairs, she checked Juliet's room. Craig's room, as she'd mentally renamed it two years before. Maybe she'd jinx him into showing.

Poinsettias, amenities, fluffed pillows. Extra fruit. Everything was in order.

Craig wasn't there.

Back downstairs again, she passed Brutus. Checked the parlor to make certain no one had snuck in while she'd been occupied upstairs. And passed Brutus a second time.

"He'd have called if he wasn't coming," she told the animal. He cocked an eye at her.

"It would help if you'd learn to speak even a word or two of English," she snapped. "Eye reading gets old."

Twenty minutes later, she was sitting on the floor, back against the huge wood door that fronted the Orange Blossom, the dog lying in her lap—or at least, as much of him as would fit.

"Some Children See Him" played throughout the downstairs. She wished it would shut up.

"Is he coming, buddy?" she asked, no longer holding panic at bay. He wouldn't do this to her, would he?

Unless he'd been in some kind of accident. Who would know to notify her?

Worry had become a constant companion in the days since she'd sent off her request to James. In the days she should have had a response and hadn't.

Had both of her soul mates stood her up?

A LONG WALK on the beach had done Craig McKellips no good at all. He was chilled. Damp. His black leather shoes and the bottoms of his black jeans were wet and caked with sand—in spite of his attempt to brush off both before climbing back into the rental car.

The trepidation plaguing him had not dissipated as he'd hoped. In fact, walking across sand he'd last traveled with Marybeth, had made matters much worse.

He was trapped. In a no win situation with no way out.

For the first time in his life, he understood why people contemplated suicide. Not only was his own happiness out of his grasp, but he saw no way to prevent destroying the peace and joy of those he cared about. Not that suicide would help that any.

He'd been walking a tightrope—a strand of which was his own making—for most of his life and after he'd carefully traversed across oceans on his precarious perch the damn thing was unraveling on him faster than he could outrun the fray.

It would have worked. Should have worked.

But for the women who hadn't cooperated with him, he could have been all—okay, most—things to both of them.

Pushing up the arm of his red and black pullover, he read a time that didn't surprise him. Marybeth would have been expecting him two hours ago.

He had to tell her. She'd left him no choice.

But did he make love to her first? Did he dare hope that if he loved her, physically, the bond between them would be strong enough to sustain them through the truth?

Hope was a commodity Craig had lost somewhere along the way.

Along with his confidence.

And his wife.

When his body started to get hard within two blocks of the Orange Blossom, he passed her street by. And, as his heart ached when he thought of her sitting there, waiting for him, or worse, thinking he wasn't coming and hadn't called, that he'd left her there like a pair of worn-out shoes, he turned back.

He needed, in the worst way, to feel her in his arms. And when he acknowledged to himself that he'd be able to coax her into them, he passed the turn a second time.

He wasn't going to use her. Didn't want to coax her. He only wanted to make love to her if she needed the lovemaking as badly as he did.

This wasn't a time for ego. Or for playing coy. Marybeth's desire for him was as powerful as his was for her. That was a fact.

And he was the only one in possession of all the facts. It was up to him to decide how best to handle this situation.

Love her first?

Or tell her first and lose any chance of ever loving her? Take away any chance she'd ever have to accept his love?

Did she need his love?

Or would it be kinder to let her hate him and get on with her life?

Would she be able to get on with her life?

She needed him. Just as he needed her.

There was no choice but to let the love bond them, to trust it to bond them. Then to face the future.

Or was he being selfish? Taking a moment before he lost a lifetime?

Back and forth he drove, finding no resolution, only the same sense of desperation that had been plaguing him for months.

He had no say in how this would end. No chance to make it good. He was just as certain of that as he was that his time was up. Life was going to take a drastic turn with or without his cooperation.

On his fourth time past her street, he turned. Stopped at the Orange Blossom and went inside.

THE MINUTE SHE SAW Craig's face, she knew something had happened. Any anger she might have conjured in the past couple of hours quickly fled.

Coming from around the registration desk—where she'd been standing since she'd seen his car turn into the driveway—she stopped just short of throwing her arms around him.

"What's wrong?"

The bag he dropped relieved some of the anxiety. He was planning to stay at least.

"Sorry I'm late," he said, not quite meeting her eyes. "I should have called."

That was it. No excuses. No explanation.

Where normally she'd have taken the hint and gladly retreated, checked him into his room as though he were no more than the guest he seemed to be pretending to be, her back stiffened and she stood her ground instead.

"Craig? Please tell me what's wrong."

"I…" As he shifted, she noticed the sand adorning hi lower half. He'd been to the beach. For a long time, by the look of things.

While she'd been worrying about him, he'd been right here in town. Something was definitely not right.

Glancing up, she saw him watching her take in his appear ance. Then their eyes met. Held. And he nodded.

"May I take my bag up first?"

Because she'd feel better knowing that he'd moved back in, as much as because she wanted to accommodate him Marybeth nodded—and wordlessly handed him the key crossing behind him to lock the front door.

"Have you eaten?" The question, directed at the back o his head, stopped him at the first step.

He seemed to be giving great consideration to a very simple question, as though weighing the ramifications of his response

"No." He hadn't turned around.

"I made snacks. If I put them out, will you eat?"

His nod seemed like a death knoll.

Marybeth lost any appetite she'd had.

WITH A LETTER BURNING the denim of the back pocket of his jeans, Craig stood in the parlor of the inn he'd begun to think of as home, fondling the dog who seemed to accept him as part of the family, waiting for his hostess to return.

Trying to calm the fire raging through his body. He was going to love her. He had to love her.

It was their only chance to have that connection before he dropped the bombshell that could sever them forever.

If he dropped it first, they'd have no chance.

And if it didn't work, if she still hated him, then at leas she'd be over him once and for all—free to find love else where. He'd have helped her to overcome her doubts where her sexuality was concerned, which would show her that her mother's tragedy hadn't damaged her in that area and allow her to open herself up to the love of another man.

Whatever man was her perfect match—the one waiting out there somewhere.

Or so he told himself.

The sideboard was set and even from a distance, he recognized some of his favorites: the meatballs made with grape jelly; the chipped beef cheese ball; pea salad.

Funny how there was always more food at these evening cocktail functions when he was here alone.

The acknowledgment was bittersweet.

When he looked back at the door to Marybeth's apartment, wondering what was keeping her, she was standing there, a bottle of wine and two glasses in her hands, watching him.

"I didn't hear you come in."

"I noticed."

Setting the glasses on the coffee table in front of the couch, Marybeth filled them both with red wine.

He watched her hands and felt them on his body, gliding over his naked back.

She filled a plate. Put it next to one of the glasses.

"Sit." The look she gave him was mixed—commanding and compassionate without completely masking the anxiety.

God, how he needed to love her. To bring the light of heaven to her eyes. Now that he knew he was going to do it, he could think of little else.

He sat.

And tried not to let her see how badly his hands were shaking. He, with all of his experience, had no idea what to do. He was fifteen again. Never having touched a woman…

She held up her glass. "Merry Christmas to a very dear friend," she toasted, tipping her glass to his.

"Merry Christmas." The warmth of those eyes with the unique violet flecks increased the pressure raging through his body. "And hello again," he added.

She smiled. The first real smile he'd seen since his arrival. An expression that kept him up nights. That he'd missed so despairingly.

"Hi."

And just like that, months' worth of defenses faded away. Months of personal work. Of strength training. All crumbled at his feet with remnants of Santa Barbara sand.

He had a meatball. And another. Telling himself that one physical gratification could substitute for another. He listened while she told him about Wendy and her family. About the baby she didn't have. About a nursery that was filled with Christmas craft tables.

Hearing the underlying pain, Craig thought about giving her the one thing she wanted most so that if the truth separated them forever, he still would have been able to help her— to leave her with something priceless and beautiful.

And knew he was getting ahead of himself.

He was going to make love to her. He couldn't do any more than that until she knew the truth.

"You aren't eating much." She licked a drop of wine from her lips.

No, he had another appetite to appease.

"Jenny and I are divorced." That had to be made clear.

Her glass clinked hard against the table. "What?"

"Neither one of us was in love with each other." It all seemed so simple, if still a bit painful, from this side of the fence.

"But…eight years…and…weren't you at least going to try a separation?"

He nodded. "We did. It took all of two weeks apart for us to realize that we could make it alone. And once we faced that truth, we no longer needed each other."

Hating how weak that made him sound—made him feel—Craig gave her the rest.

"We were two lonely people, afraid that the world wasn't ever going to understand us and so we were going to spend our lives alone. We were using each other to avoid that outcome. And in the meantime, neither of us was really living…or doing anything we really wanted to do, except in our work. We were settling. Enabling each other to settle."

"Wow." She was staring at him. "Have you heard from her? Is she doing okay?"

"She's back in France, where she really longed to be but wouldn't say so. Dating someone she knew before. A son of friends of her parents. We still talk every couple of weeks and his name has become about every other word for her."

"In a healthy way? Or do you think she's just switching her dependency on you to him?"

"My ex-wife, the one who always put work first, sounds like a giddy schoolgirl. She's head over heels in love."

"How does that make you feel?"

Empty glass in hand, Craig studied the crystal stem. "Truthfully?"

She nodded.

"Relieved." And that shamed him, too. Eight years of marriage and all he could feel, at the thought of his ex-wife in the arms of another man, was relief that he didn't have to try to satisfy her himself.

Frowning, Marybeth sat back. "So…is there someone else?"

He'd just received his opening.

Red liquid filled the glass in his hand. He welcomed the distraction. The false sense of help.

He welcomed the promise of pain's demise—no matter how temporary.

God help him, he was far, far, far from perfect. But he was a man who did the right thing as soon as he knew what it was.

His dad was the destroyer. He was the savior.

He'd always been a man of integrity—a man who did what he said he was going to do.

What about a man who lived two lives?

He was his father.

Except that he had the best of intentions. All he'd ever wanted to do was help.

Would any of that make a difference when he faced himself at the end of this lifetime?

"Craig? If you're here to tell me that, now that you're free, you find that you have no interest in me, that's okay."

Gaze flying to hers, Craig almost choked on his wine. If she actually thought that, he was better at duplicity than he'd thought. Better than he'd ever wanted to be.

"It's clear that, while a part of you wants to be here, another part very clearly doesn't," she was saying, as he was trying to figure out how to start making love to her. "The way you arrived—not only late, but…you know…not yourself—I just don't want you to feel like you owe me anything. You don't. At all. If I was a grass is greener on the other side kind of thing that helped you get out of a bad place or helped you see that the place was bad, then that's okay. I'm good with that."

If anything was his undoing—if there was anything left of him to undo—the sincerity in her eyes was it. She meant every word she said. As he'd always known, Marybeth Lawson was a very special woman. One of a kind.

Would she understand that he'd done everything for her? Would she be able to see that his actions were a product of how much he cared?

He didn't know what to say. How to respond. In all of his various scenarios of this moment, her thinking he didn't want her had never once taken stage.

"I…"

"It's okay." Her hand against him made his mouth dry. He could count the number of times they'd touched. Twice. And had relived the moments every day since. "I'm not going to fall apart on you, or—"

"You're wrong." The words came. Without plan of any kind. And that's when he knew there'd never been a decision for him to make. That this was out of his hands, regardless of what he thought. "I've never wanted a woman more than I want you."

Truth. Bald. Unadorned. Right or wrong, there it was.

Her hand on his became a death grip. "Then…"

"I want you to know how much you mean to me," he said, staring her straight in the eye. "I am so in love with you I can't think straight. I have been, forever, it seems. It's important that you believe that."

"I do," she said, lips trembling. "Because I feel the same way."

No. This wasn't about her giving of herself. This was about him giving. About her taking.

"You don't know anything about me."

"Baloney. I know your heart and that's all that matters. Even if I didn't feel the real you every time I'm with you, I see you in your art. You're gifted, Craig. You have the ability to reach inside yourself and show the rest of us things about the world that we might otherwise miss. And you do so without thought for personal gain, or recognition or ego building.

"You move quietly through the world, observing and giving us the best things that we'd otherwise miss in our own bumblings through everyday life."

He could hardly swallow the wine he gulped, needing her to stop before she said any more words she'd later take back.

"But that's not how I know you," she said, her gaze growing soft, filling with a sensual softness, a maturity, he'd never seen there before. His penis was so hard he contemplated a cold shower so he could hang on long enough to be capable of giving her the pleasure she deserved.

"I know you because of all the men I've dated—and there have now been more than I want to count—not one of them has brought forth any deeper feeling at all. I've not once felt the hint of sexual desire. Or even a mild attraction. I don't need to be around them or care if I ever see them again. I never think about them.

"You are the only man who has ever had the ability to rouse emotion in me. The only man I feel safe with…" She was leaning closer as she spoke, her voice drifting lower. "The only man I've ever dared do this with…"

He'd known it was coming. He had to have known. But when her lips touched his, Craig felt the shock all the way through his system. Heart. Mind. Body.

He was electrocuted. Impacted beyond rational thought.

CHAPTER TWENTY-ONE

OPENING HIS MOUTH, Craig took her tongue inside him. Tasting her. Allowing her to taste him. Fully. A beginning of what was to come. He had much to teach her. Much to show her. Much to learn, he suspected.

Breathing with frenzied hunger, she didn't seem to need his tutoring. She devoured his mouth—her innocent hunger more of a turn-on than any practiced passion had ever been.

"Touch me, please." Her plea made him ache.

With hands on either side of her face, Craig was jolted by the moisture his palms encountered.

She was crying.

"I'm scared," she said, without any coyness. "I'm almost thirty years old and I don't know what it feels like to lie in a man's arms. To have his hands on my breasts. I don't know what's on the other end of this painful hunger you make me feel. Every time I think of you, I ache for more. For something I don't even know."

She hiccuped.

"Shh," Craig whispered, pulling her tenderly toward him, kissing the tears from her cheeks.

"I'm afraid there's something wrong with me," she said. "I'm some kind of nymphomaniac when you're around and—"

"What you're feeling is perfectly natural," he assured her quietly, suffused with a strength that was not his own as he held back the fire that raged within him. "If you'd felt it at fifteen, in a younger version, you'd be more equipped to recognize it now. But I promise you, there's nothing wrong with what you're feeling."

"Love me, Craig. Please. I don't care if you're leaving after Christmas and never seeing me again. I need this. I need you."

Which was exactly what he'd known. What he'd been telling himself. Loving her might be his last gift to her.

And he was going to do it well. Give it all.

Drunk on her, on a desire too long denied, driven by a body that was in so much pain he could hardly move without pressing it against her, Craig wondered if maybe this was fate, pushing him in a direction he couldn't see, but one that was right.

She slid her hands beneath his sweater, running her fingers through the hair on his chest, finding his nipples.

"Oh, baby." He groaned, pulling her down to the couch on top of him. "You feel so damned good."

"Teach me, Craig. Show me how to make love."

"I'm going to," he promised her. "I'm going to love you until every single part of your body knows what it feels like to be touched by a man. By me."

"I'm getting wet down there," she told him, sounding half panicked, half wild as she straddled his leg.

He lifted his leg, pressing it into her, taking her with him as he spun into a world of passion, where anything goes as long as it was the two of them. He'd had sex hundreds of times. Had all the experience, the know-how, the ideas she could possibly need or want—and yet being with her was like the first time.

It felt different. Even physically. His penis was harder, fuller. His entire body tensed with the need to be inside her. And his hands ached to touch her softly, gently, to explore all of her long before he brought either of them to release.

MARYBETH wasn't kidding herself. She knew full well that Craig wasn't around to stay. He'd told her long ago, that even without Jenny, he'd never commit to her.

She might be able to change his mind.

And maybe not.

At the moment, none of that mattered. Craig might be the only man in her life who'd be able to arouse these feelings. She needed him. Even if he was hers only for this one brief moment. She didn't want to live her whole life without having experienced the sweet pains and ecstasies of passion.

His kisses were heaven and home at the same time. She recognized the smell of him, the taste of him, as though she'd known him forever. Been tasting him forever. He didn't hold back, demanding all she had to give and finding more. The roof of her mouth, the top of her tongue, he took his time with her, touching her. Sucking in air, he ran his hands along her back, down to the edge of her hips and up, trailing along her sides.

Her nerves tingled in anticipation of what he was going to do to her. Take off her sweater and jeans. Unhook her bra. Pull down her panties. See her down there. Touch her. The very idea of it excited her beyond anything she'd ever known before.

As he continued to kiss her lips, her neck, her cheeks and eyelids, his hands moved up and down her sides, skimming closer and closer to breasts that throbbed with need. Her thighs quivered as she considered his imminent invasion and her hips rose of their own accord, seeking hardness, strength.

She almost exploded out of her skin when his hand cupped her breast through her sweater, her nipple sending shock waves through her system and down to the warmth between her legs.

"I had no idea," she said, breaking away to gasp in air.

"Do you want to stop?" She almost didn't recognize his ragged voice.

"No!" She hadn't meant to sound so sharp. "Not at all," she

managed to say in a more congenial tone. "I just, honestly, I had no idea that my…up there…that they were, you know, that they'd…"

"I have a feeling you're in for a few pleasant surprises," he told her with a warm look and chuckle to match, sending another wave of desire flooding downward.

"At the rate we're going, I'm going to be done before we've really begun," she said, needing to know what *done* felt like, but afraid of missing out on the getting there.

"Ah, surprise number two," he said. "You're a woman. You don't have to be done. You're going to have more than one orgasm before I'm done with you tonight."

Sounded delicious. Sinful. Better than she'd imagined she'd ever feel in this lifetime. She could happily die right here in Craig's arms. "I am?" she managed to ask, wriggling her body against his.

"Mmm-hmm." He rolled her over and settled half on top of her. He looked from her face, down to her breasts, back up, then down again. "You ready for more?"

"Yeah." And no. She licked her lips, apprehensive and tense with need. She wanted to savor. To prepare.

She'd heard it hurt.

The undeniable male muscle pushing up against her thigh felt huge.

"I'm going to pull your sweater up."

"Okay."

And when he reached for the edges, she lifted off of the couch to facilitate, shivering as the cool air reached her skin—as her skin became exposed to a man's sight for the first time in her life.

Judging by the intense glint in his eyes, the shaking of his hands, he liked what he was revealing.

And before she could warn herself, remind herself what was coming, her bra-clad breasts were free, poking up at him, exposed. Tossing her sweater aside, he was staring at her cleavage. Bent to kiss it.

And unclasped her bra at the same time.

"Smooth move," she half choked, resisting the automatic impulse to cover herself with her arms.

She lay with her arms at her sides, instead. Allowing him to lift her bra off her breasts, slide it down her arms and toss it aside. She allowed him to look at her fully.

And when he lifted a hand, she allowed him to take her nipple in between his fingers.

She allowed him to do all kinds of things to her body that she'd never imagined. Anything he wanted to do. He suckled her breasts, nipping lightly. He suckled the skin of her neck. Explored her belly button with his tongue.

He caressed her spine, her head, the undersides of her arms, following his fingers with kisses that were sometimes light, sometimes accompanied by his tongue and always heavenly.

"You're making me a wanton slut," she panted.

"Don't ever say that," he said. "There's nothing slutty about you. What you're feeling is the natural and healthy desire that comes with being a woman who's with the man she wants."

"So why are you so calm?" Other than some shaking fingers, a bit of rough breathing, he seemed almost unaffected, while she was coming up off the couch. Whimpering with need.

Embarrassing the heck out of herself.

And he hadn't even touched her jeans yet.

"Calm?" Craig sounded strangled all of a sudden. Grabbing her hand, he took it to the fly of his jeans, opening it over him and pressing himself against her palm. "Does this feel calm to you?"

"It feels…large." His penis was throbbing. Somehow she hadn't expected that.

He burst out with laughter. "It is…large," he mimicked her. "So large it hurts. It's taking everything I have to control the urge to sink it into you and explode until I die."

"Then why don't you?" she asked, smiling up at him. "I'm okay with that. Except for the dying part."

"Because as soon as I come, I'm going to be limp as a noodle and I have much business to tend to before then."

"Oh." Her cheeks burned. Her legs opened. Not a ladylike position at all. She spread them farther.

"You need to be touched down there, don't you?"

Looking in Craig's eyes, Marybeth was no longer embarrassed. They were partners on this odd journey, this bizarre dance of sensation and heart connection. "Yes, I do," she told him, not completely sure what she was admitting—or asking for.

"Badly?"

"I think so."

"Then let's do something about that, shall we?"

He was watching her, not moving, as though, even now, after she'd touched his penis, had him to the point of craziness, he was willing to stop at the slightest sign that she wanted him to do so.

She might be inexperienced, but she knew enough to realize how difficult that would be for him.

"Please do something about that," she whispered, her gaze locked with his.

"You're sure?"

"I've never been more sure about anything in my life." Except her friendship with James.

With a start, she realized that this was the first time since she'd sat down with Craig that evening that she'd even thought of James.

Uncomfortable with the discovery, but understanding how, when she was about to embark on the most intimate personal experience of her life, she'd think of James.

He was the good voice in her head.

What scared the hell out of her was the knowledge that somehow, in the past hour—or maybe over the past two years—Craig had begun to mean as much to her as James did.

She hadn't thought anyone else would ever get that close to her.

HE LOVED HER WELL. For the rest of the evening and into the night. At some point Brutus ambled off to lay guard in the kitchen, where he stayed even when Craig, naked and sated and supposed to be weak and tired, carried Marybeth into her bedroom, to make love to her all over again.

She'd experienced feelings, reactions she'd said she'd not known were possible to feel.

And he'd reached heretofore impossible heights, as well— satisfaction seemingly only a temporary resting place, not the end of the night.

Lying with her in his arms, sometime after midnight, he could no longer ignore the daylight that was going to arrive, no matter how determined they were to pretend that it wasn't.

He wasn't sorry about the night. But moving forward was going to be harder now than he'd ever imagined.

And he'd already known telling Marybeth what he'd come to tell her, watching her turn away from him, leaving her, was going to be the hardest thing he'd ever done.

"We need to talk."

"Now?"

If he had his way, he'd wait forever. But then he knew what they were facing. She had a right to know as much.

"It's important. Critically important." He regretted the

condoms he'd used—wished he could at least hope that he'd given her the baby she wanted.

She stirred against him, her hair tickling the underside of his chin in a way he'd remember over and over in the years to come. He was cataloging everything, from the sound and feel of her breathing, to the smell of her sheets, to hoard as memories as he lived out his life.

"What you're going to tell me—it's not good, is it?"

"No."

"It's going to hurt."

"Yes."

"A lot."

"Yes."

"Then please, can we have just these few days? Can we wait until after Christmas? Enjoy the holiday together? Make a good memory? After that I'll listen to whatever you have to tell me."

She was handing him respite—a chance to live a joy beyond his imagination for a few days, which was more than he'd dared hope.

"You wouldn't say that if you knew what I have to tell you."

"You've told me that much, so now it's my choice, isn't it?"

Now that he'd come to the realization that he had to come clean—that he had to tell her everything—he couldn't rest until she knew. Until she could protect herself. "I don't think so."

The vulnerable, yet determined expression on Marybeth's face as she sat up was clear, even in the muted light from the moon shining in the window across the room.

"Don't hurt me on the holiday, Craig. Please. Today is Christmas Eve. Tomorrow's Christmas. The world can wait two days, can't it?" She didn't wait for an answer. "Everything is always so much more acute during these couple of days. Life stops for everyone to take time off to be with whoever is most special to them and the quiet can be deafening when you don't have someone that special in your life.

"As I know you know."

He did. Completely.

"Please wait until life is in full swing again, until I can lose myself out in a busy world if I have to."

He opened his mouth to capitulate and she put a finger over his lips. "Please. I know I'm not being fair, but you'd planned to stay so I know I'm not taking you away from anything else. Right?"

"I have nowhere else to be."

"I've had enough hard Christmases to last me a lifetime, Craig." Her voice had softened. "So maybe I'm playing the poor-me card here, but I'm begging now, give me until after Christmas and I'll listen to whatever you have to say."

The day before Christmas or the day after, his news would tell the same. Two days wasn't going to change it.

"I can't guarantee that I'll manage to stay upstairs in my bed all alone now that I've tasted this heaven," he warned.

"I can't guarantee you'd be all alone," she returned. "You're forgetting, I have a key to your room."

"Okay." He pulled her back down on top of him, settling her head against his chest. "But first thing on Friday morning, we talk. Deal?"

"Deal."

CHAPTER TWENTY-TWO

MARYBETH was no stranger to bad news. Nor to the fact that it could leave devastating changes in its wake. She wasn't naive, or stupid enough to pretend that those two days with Craig bore any resemblance to reality. Or to ignore the fact that she was going to need internal resources to get through whatever it was he had to tell her. He thought it was bad.

And he knew her pretty well.

She also wasn't stupid enough to turn her back on an unexpected gift. For the next two days, Marybeth discovered her womanhood. Not just in bed, or while she and Craig were touching—which they did almost constantly—but when they were across the room from each other, as well. Riding in the car. Or sitting in church on Christmas Eve. There was a certain power inherent in being a woman wanted by a man.

And a feeling of excitement, of enticement and desire and love grew stronger in the sharing.

She enjoyed the days for what they were—the best Christmas holiday she'd ever had. A taste of pure joy.

A collection of perfect moments.

"I can't believe you found these, or that you thought to get them," she said Christmas night as they sat in the parlor, the tree providing the only light in the room. She was holding the series of 1959 *I Love Lucy* comic books he'd given her that morning over breakfast.

"I had no idea you knew I loved this show and Lucy."

"You had a mug on your drain board when I was here last year. And the calendar at check-in is always a Lucy calendar."

And this was why she loved this man.

And James.

They noticed life.

THE TICKING CLOCK grew increasingly louder in Craig's mind as Christmas night drew to a close. He had one more night to sleep with Marybeth Lawson.

And then life was going to intervene.

He touched her with less gentleness that night, less tenderness, but no less love. Driven by a desperate passion that seemed to consume her, as well, he barely had time to sheath himself with another condom before they joined together again and again, faster and faster, as though they could outrun the time that was running out.

He rolled over and she was on top of him, moving her body up and down on his, letting him watch it all, and when he came, the cry that ripped out of him was barely recognizable.

It was only when she froze that he realized what he'd said.

MARYBETH WAS OUT of the bed and across the room, staring at the man half lying there, buck naked, with horror coursing through her. She knew every inch of his body and yet it was as though she'd never seen him before.

Because she hadn't.

"You called me Candy."

The resigned look in his eyes told her the secret he'd been keeping.

And she didn't want to know.

Ever.

He didn't speak, but she didn't need the confirmation. Only one other person, dead or alive, knew that name. It had been made up specifically for them. To hide them from the world. From everyone but each other.

"I…" Cold, light-headed, she didn't know what to say. What to do. Where to look.

Standing there naked didn't seem like a good idea, yet she couldn't figure out how to move.

Or where.

"I…can't…"

She'd dreamed of this moment for half of her life. And never, ever had it been this bad. Not even when he'd denied her requests to meet. Either time.

"James." The word found its way out of her—feeling no better in the telling than it had been trapped inside.

"Yes."

James. Her James. The one human being she could trust. Had trusted with every single ounce of her being. The one person with whom she'd felt safe. Until Craig.

And now both of them…

Betrayal wasn't new to her, after all. She'd been betrayed by a world that had allowed a fiend to enter her home, rape her mother, kill her and leave her soaked in blood to greet a twelve-year-old girl after school.

She'd been betrayed by the father who'd been unable to recover enough to be a father to her.

Staring in horror, she watched Craig—James, whoever he was—pull on the jeans she'd so impatiently pulled off him hours before.

"Marybeth…"

"Damn you to hell." She had nothing better to give him.

Seeming to recognize that, to know her so well when she felt as though she didn't know him at all—had never known him—the man turned and left the room, leaving her all alone in the darkness of her own hell.

SHE MANAGED TO DON a pair of pajamas. Mostly, she thought, because Brutus was staring at her as though he expected her to do something and this was about all she could handle.

Eventually, she made her way to her sitting room. The bed was too damning, her emotions too raw and painful for her to get anywhere near the sheets she'd shared with her own personal Judas.

The sobs, when they came, were like everything else about this night. Out of control. There, whether she wanted them or not. Ripping her apart from the inside out. She was choking herself and still, they wouldn't stop.

"Put your head between your knees."

The words came out of the darkness, all knowing, instructing. On the verge of passing out, Marybeth followed the directive.

And when the hysteria subsided, she stared into the corner from whence the voice had come, her eyes adjusting to the dark enough to make out an outline she'd never forget. With one hundred years of faithful and determined trying, she was never going to forget the man.

Or what he'd done to her.

"How long have you been there?" As if it mattered. Seventeen years too long for one of him. Two years too long for the other.

"I never left."

"You aren't welcome here."

"I know. But I'm not leaving you alone in the dark."

"I'd rather be alone than be anywhere near you."

"I know."

"Can't you come up with anything more original to say?"

Venom spewed from her, an anger so deep, so intense, she couldn't stem its flow. "Come on, *James,* you always have the perfect answer. You know it all. Right? Get out of my house. Out of my sight. You make me sick."

The words continued tumbling one after the other, until *she* was making her sick.

He didn't move, didn't even seem to flinch. His skin was a lot thicker than she'd ever realized.

"Why are you still here?"

"Because I'm not leaving you alone."

"I'm not a baby."

"I know exactly who and what you are." His voice was soft. Compassionate.

"Don't humor me."

"I wouldn't dare."

"No, you'd just dare to betray me. That's a lot better, huh?" If she could stay angry enough, long enough, maybe she could hate him. "You. Of all people."

She started to cry again. Quietly. Uncaring that he saw. Knew.

"I tried to tell you."

"Yeah, right. Three days ago. I'm not upset about that, Craig. James. Whoever you are." The bitterness in her voice hurt to hear. Hurt even worse to feel. "I asked for these few days. But how do you explain two years of deception? I feel like such a fool."

No wonder Craig had been able to get through her defenses. No wonder he'd been different from the very beginning. Some part of her had recognized him.

Which meant that part of her had betrayed her, too. She'd recognized him, but hadn't conveyed the danger to herself. The duplicity. Hadn't had any inkling, any instinct or premonition, that this man was going to hurt her.

Could hurt her.

Would hurt her.

Not seventeen years ago. Not two years ago. Not two hours ago.

She stared across at him, dressed in only the jeans he'd pulled on, sitting in the corner in her great-aunt's favorite chair, watching her.

"Why don't you go?"

"Because I can't."

"Can't? What does that mean?"

"I love you, Candy. I always have. You know that. I know that. And you know me well enough to know that I can't desert you. Not ever. No matter what."

He looked like Craig. Used Craig's voice.

And spoke to her like seventeen years' worth of letters come to life.

"James."

"Yes."

"My James."

"Yes."

"Sitting here, in my living room. Tangible. Alive."

"Yes."

"Flesh and blood."

"I've always been that."

The tears came again as the reality of her greatest dream came to life. In the form of a nightmare. Nothing made sense. Not life. Or death. No reason. Or feeling.

"James?" The cry was from someplace deep within—a lost child needing more than she could understand. A woman with a damaged heart.

Panic struck as she imagined him gone, doing as she'd bid and walking out of her life as stealthily as he'd come in. He was a change artist. A trickster.

And he was her salvation.

Rising Marybeth approached him, watching, half afraid he'd disappear before her eyes if she so much as blinked. "James?" she asked again, dropping down on her knees before him.

"Yes."

"Hold me? Please?"

It didn't mean anything, just a salve that would allow her to pass through the moment. A salve that she needed desperately enough to beg for it.

"Take me to bed and hold me until the light comes?"

Without a sound he stood. Gathered her in his arms as though she was a child again. Safe. Secure. In the arms of one who loved her unconditionally.

And when he lay with her, cradling her body within the protective curve of his, she closed her eyes and, breathing in his scent, losing herself in the essence of her James, she fell asleep.

CRAIG DIDN'T close his eyes. For the rest of that night he hardly blinked. He didn't want to miss a minute of watching Marybeth sleep, of knowing that she was safe. Loved. Finding a measure of peace.

The morrow would come. He didn't deceive himself into thinking that her body pressed so trustingly against his meant anything more than that she'd been at the end of her ability to cope alone.

But she'd regain her strength. He understood that. Welcomed it.

As much as he dreaded what would come next.

She awoke at the first light of dawn. He could tell, not so much by the change in her breathing, but in the way she stiffened against him—remembering, he'd guess.

"Is Craig McKellips your real name?"

"James is my real name."

"And Craig is the name you were given that day in court. The name the world knows you by."

"Yes."

She was still lying plastered to his side, but there was no doubting the walls between them.

"When did you first decide to deceive me?"

"I never made that decision."

"Oh, the whole not telling me thing just happened without your knowing?" The sarcasm was back. "I'm sorry," she added before he could respond. "That's not like me."

"I realize that," he said, finding it impossible to do anything but love her. With all of his heart.

A heart that no one but she had ever known.

She moved only enough to look at him. "Why, James?"

There were so many answers to give her. True and valid answers. But only one that was ever going to explain in a way she'd fully understand.

"I can't believe this," she said when he didn't come up with an immediate response. "I'd rather have found out you were a murderer or something. Because you are, you know, only instead of killing someone I've never met, you murdered the most sacred thing of all. My ability to trust you."

He couldn't argue with her. He'd known this was coming. He knew her. Probably as well as she knew herself.

The way she'd known him, not that she'd believe anything she thought she knew about him now.

"I don't blame you for the past few days," she said. "You tried your best to come clean, I'll give you that. What kills me, kills us, is the past two years. All the times you had a chance to say something. I just don't get it. This isn't the James I know.

"Knew," she amended. "You deliberately deceived me. I—" She shook her head, sounding lost. Alone. Exactly what he'd spent the majority of his life trying to avoid. "Why would you do such a thing? How could you do it? Didn't we mean anything to you?"

"Of course we did. Still do. You're the best part of me, Marybeth. You always have been."

"Don't lie to me."

The fact that he deserved her doubt didn't ease the pain of being in possession of it.

"I have never lied to you except by omission," he said. "Every word I've ever given you—written and otherwise—has been complete truth."

"Your wife's name is Jenny."

"Was."

"James is divorced?" She seemed to be struggling with the idea of the two men becoming one. He didn't blame her. He'd spent so much of his life with dual identities—the real him that she knew, and the him that the rest of the world saw—that he wasn't sure he knew how to blend the two.

"I'm divorced, yes."

"Because of me? You…James was going to tell his wife about me in an attempt to be more fully connected to her."

"I was going to after the trial separation. I never got the chance. Never needed the chance."

"So the two weeks…and the realization you both had about not being in love, about hiding behind each other, was true?"

"Every word."

"And…you…" She sat up, staring at him. "James is an artist." The words were half statement, half question.

"Yep."

And then she stilled, as though remembering something else.

"Your father's in prison."

He tensed. "Yes."

"He writes to you, but you never read his letters."

"Right."

"Why?"

There it was, a second time. And he knew her well enough to know the question would continue to come until she had the answer. The full answer. All of it.

He opened his mouth in spite of the fact that he was sealing their fate.

CHAPTER TWENTY-THREE

"I'LL GET TO THE MAN who fathered me, but if you're ready to listen, I'd like to explain some other things, first."

"Go ahead."

"Two years ago, when I first came to see you, I didn't fully understand myself why. I'd seen the ad in the brochure, like I told you, recognized the address of the Orange Blossom. And once I knew you were running a bed-and-breakfast, I knew I had a way to see you from afar. That was all I could think about. I see now that it was partially because of my own searching. I needed something bigger than myself to help me see myself. You were it. The love we shared was it."

"Which is as it should have been." Even now Marybeth couldn't deny that truth.

"But it was more than that. I was worried about you—to the point of having problems focusing on other things. Your dad had died, you had no one close in your life. I was afraid that we'd saved you all these years, only for you to lose yourself in the end."

All things he'd already told her. Things she'd taken to heart, believed, the first time she'd heard them.

She didn't want to believe them now. As soon as she could figure out a way to make them not ring true.

"Still, I was afraid for us to meet for all the reasons I told you. You needed me, James, the guy who never judged, who had no expectations. You needed that safe outlet, a place to go where you could say anything. I needed you, too, but I can swear to you that at that time, I was thinking about how much you'd told me you relied on my presence in your life. If we met, if expectations and judgments appeared, as is natural in human interaction, if you lost your ability to talk to me without filtering, I was afraid you'd be so completely trapped inside there'd be no way out."

"You were my way out." That was no secret, either.

"Exactly. So, at a time when I'm worried about you sliding back inside, how could I risk sending you there permanently?"

His logic made sense. In a James kind of way.

Which was the way that always spoke to her most.

"I was also afraid that if we met, other feelings might get in the way and mess things up."

"Other feelings?" But she knew what he was talking about. She was lying naked in the bed with him.

He covered her breast and her nipple hardened instantly. "Need I say more?"

"I told Craig about my mother."

"Something you'd never told me before," he acknowledged, and she wondered now if that had hurt him.

"I told him about you," she reminded him.

"You told me about me," he shot back. "I understood, sweetie, that everything you gave to Craig, you were subconsciously giving to James."

Maybe. Or maybe she'd fallen in love twice—with two different parts of the same man. So did that mean that love was duplicitous? Easily fooled? Or had love recognized the sameness in the man even when she hadn't?

It was a question she would have taken straight to a letter to James.

"I just wanted to make certain that you were okay. I wanted

to make certain that if there was anything I could do to help, I did it. Then I was going to fade away—a guest who'd come and gone—and you'd never have been the wiser."

"So what happened?"

James pulled her close to face him, their heads side by side on the pillow. She liked being there far too much.

"This happened," he said, his eyes bloodshot, lined with fatigue, yet completely alert. "As much as I promised myself I'd stay away from you, you kept calling me back. Your power over me was much stronger than any discipline I had over myself, or so I thought. I realize now that it was the love calling me back. You know, you can run but you can't hide."

She couldn't fall for this. He had all the right words, but then, she knew that. She'd been on the receiving end of James's words for seventeen years. But what did they mean, really? Where did the deception end and the truth begin?

How could she ever trust him again?

"Just for informational purposes, why were you so all fired bent on telling me the truth now? What changed? Other than your divorce?"

"My divorce had nothing to do with this. Or us."

"Then what changed? Why did you suddenly decide that you could risk my losing your support? Obviously you know me well. You knew that once I knew you'd lied to me, I'd think that what we'd shared was fantasy."

"I knew I was going to lose you."

A crazy conversation to have lying in bed, skin to skin, face-to-face.

"So suddenly this great love you have for me, this need to make certain that I always had your support, your protection, this need to preserve our unconditional acceptance of each other, is no longer there?"

"Oh, sweetie, it's there." She wanted to tell him not to call her that. And she would. Eventually.

"It was that last letter," he continued. And with a flood of clarity, she put more pieces together. She'd asked this man to donate sperm for her baby.

She'd wanted to have his child.

Because Craig was James.

"You didn't answer the letter."

"This was my answer. Your letter convinced me that you'd been right all along. The safe place I was trying so painstakingly to preserve wasn't real enough to survive life. You needed more. And this time, now that I didn't have Jenny to hide behind, now that I knew I had been hiding, now that I knew you, I realized that in addition to the other things keeping us apart, I was just plain scared."

"Of what?"

"Loving and losing again." He frowned. "Pretty lame, huh? After all this, after pushing you for so many years to step up and live life, to risk, I find that all along, you were the brave one, forging ahead, and I was the coward."

"Hardly a coward," she told him. "You tried marriage. I didn't even date."

"I tried it with the wrong person."

So did that mean she'd been right all along in not dating? That there'd been nothing wrong with her; she'd simply been in love with a man she couldn't have because he wouldn't meet her?

Was it possible to not only love someone, but to be in love with them through paper and pen? What constituted a person? And how encompassing was love? Could it travel across states, stay alive with no physical presence?

More James questions.

"When I read that you wanted me to father your child, I couldn't tell you no. But I could never father your child without letting you know the truth," James said with Craig's voice. "I knew you by then. I'd have to be by your side, taking you to the doctor, in the delivery room. I'd have to be a father to our child. And all that aside, once I knew I was wrong in my thinking, my only choice was to make it right."

"I know the truth," she said, fighting back more fear, "and things have never been worse between us."

"In some ways, but they're more real now than ever before."

"Some things were real." At least for her.

"The love was real," he said. "And every word I ever said to you was real."

She wanted to believe that. "It's the things you don't say that I have to watch out for."

And there was the bald truth. The frightening truth. How could you protect yourself from that which you didn't know existed?

"You said you'd get to the man who fathered you," she reminded him now, looking for anything, everything that she didn't know about him. Looking for an escape from the image of him as the father of her child. "Why don't you read his letters?"

Craig-James hugged her close, squeezing her so tightly she almost couldn't breathe. And then he got up. Dressed.

Without a word, Marybeth did the same. Foreboding froze her heart. Something was horribly wrong here—much more wrong than the man she'd trusted above all others deceiving her.

An hour ago, she wouldn't have thought anything could be worse than that.

She needed coffee. Brutus. Whatever was about to come, James wasn't going to be able to make it better.

CRAIG FOLLOWED Marybeth to the kitchen. Watched as Brutus came in his pet door from the gated grass area reserved for his business.

While she made coffee, set the table with fruit and rolls that neither of them were going to eat, he started to talk.

"The first twelve years of my life were ideal," he told her. Something else they had in common. "Like you, I was an only child. My parents and I were close, did everything together as a family—especially me and my dad. He taught me to shoot, to golf. He took me to the batting cages every Saturday."

"In the spring and summer," she intervened, putting plates and napkins on the table. "Obviously you can't golf or bat in the snow."

"I didn't live in Colorado then."

"Oh. Where were you?"

"Here. In California."

She turned from the counter, looked at him. "Where?"

"Between here and L.A."

"You lived that close to me?" The frown on her face told him she didn't have a clue what was coming. And he had no way to break this one easy.

Marybeth added jam to the table, between the bowl of strawberries and the basket of rolls.

"Then, when I was twelve, it all fell apart," he said as they sat. "One day, while we were at the dinner table, there was a knock on the door. It was the police. They had a warrant for my dad's arrest."

"Oh, my God." The coffee carafe suspended in midair, she stared at him. "That was right before we met. And your mother…and…"

She stopped.

"Your mother was raped and your father was arrested all in the same year?"

"My mother was never raped."

"But…of course she was. We…that's how we met."

She'd gone white. Craig had never hated more who he

was. And everything his life had become. Never wished more that he'd never been born.

How could something that had started out as a young man's way to pay for his father's mistakes, turn so god-awful wrong?

"The counseling was for kids whose parents had been involved in rape."

"Yeah." She nodded, staring at him. "Victims of rape."

"The kids are all considered victims of rape. The parents weren't all victims."

"What are you saying? That your father was involved with rape but wasn't a victim?"

"Yes." He held her gaze as she processed that, trying with every ounce of strength he had to help her hold on. To give her the energy she was going to need to get through this.

"He was a rapist?"

"Yes."

"Your father is a rapist?" she said again, as though to be perfectly clear.

"Yes."

"Your mother and you—you guys had no idea?"

"None. I didn't believe it for months," he told her, remembering those weeks of agony while the papers tore his beloved father to shreds and he continued to believe in the man who was his hero. "He lived a double life."

"How…how many…were there?"

"He was convicted on seven counts." Of rape, that was. Then there was the murder. Only one of those. The critical one.

Sick to his stomach, Craig took Marybeth's hand. "There's more."

"No," she said, and then, more loudly, "no." Her eyes were glazed, wild, as she looked anywhere but at him, and then straight at him. She tried to pull her hand away. She'd guessed.

Or feared that she had.

"He's the man who killed your mom, sweet Candy. That's why I wrote to you, specifically, all those years ago. I had some wild idea that I'd spend the rest of my life making up for my father's mistakes. From the moment I first heard your name, I dedicated my life to being there for you, supporting you, no matter what."

It all sounded so childish now.

Not that it mattered. He was fairly certain Marybeth wasn't hearing a word he said.

"Your father raped my mother. He killed her." Her lips moved. The sound that came out had no inflection at all.

"Yes."

"He's still alive." Funny, he would have predicted that would be the first thing she'd say. "I'd been hoping all these years that he was dead."

She wasn't the only one. "I know."

She glanced up at him and for the first time Craig saw firsthand the meaning of eyes that were dead looking. "You've never written to him? Never answered a single letter?"

"Not since the day I heard him admit that he'd done what they said. He tried to explain, to ask me to understand that he had something wrong inside him. I didn't want to hear it. Still don't. If that makes me unforgiving, an S.O.B., close-minded, so be it."

"All these years…" Her shoulders drooped. "You've been my mother's killer's son."

It sounded worse coming from her than it had ever sounded in his head.

"You've known…"

He didn't need to say anything. She was putting it all together.

"When you were thirteen, okay, I can understand. But at sixteen? Eighteen? Twenty? You never thought to tell me? You and I, we've been living a lie, a horrible, despicable lie, for seventeen years."

They'd been living with deception. His deception. Which was about the same thing as lying.

"I thought about telling you, many times," he said. If she had any idea how many sleepless nights he'd had over the years, trying to figure out the best thing to do where she was concerned. "But why?" Replaying a million conversations he'd had with himself, he said, "If I told you, you'd lose the best friend you'd ever had. You told me again and again how much I helped you, how much I meant to you, how you were able to move on, have a good life because I was there, sharing things with you. Why would I ruin that for no good purpose? Time and again I'd go back to my original goal—to be there for you, to support you for the rest of your life. If you knew who I was, who my father was, you'd never be able to take comfort from me. There didn't seem to be any reason you'd have to know—and a very good reason why you shouldn't know. It would have worked, as long as we didn't meet. To my way of thinking we could have continued for the rest of our lives and only good would be gained."

And they could have if he'd only kept his ass out of Santa Barbara. He'd been right from the beginning after all. Looking at her, lost, suffering, angry, alone, he had to wonder what good had been served, now, in telling her the truth.

"And then you came here," she said.

"Right."

"I…" She shook her head. "I have to shower. To think. Would you mind if I had some time alone?"

Of course he minded. Tremendously. "I—"

"Please, Craig…James. I need to be alone."

And that's when he knew that she was going to be all right.

They'd raised her well, he and she. She was strong. Smart. Capable. She'd be able to take care of herself now.

And she said as much an hour later when she asked him, in the kindest way possible, to pack his bag and leave her home.

She was going to be fine. And that had been his goal all along.

He left without another word.

Left without his heart.

Wednesday, December 31, 2008

She didn't own cold weather clothes.

Shivering in the cab line at the Denver airport, wishing she had boots that were actually made to keep out the snow seeping through her black suede fashion accessory, Marybeth tried to keep her mind on easy things, like gray skies. Clouds. Freezing to death.

She climbed into the cab. Rattled off the address she knew by heart—remembering it just as she remembered every single address for every place James had lived during the past seventeen years. Knowing his address meant access to him.

"How long will it take us to get there?" she asked the female cabbie who looked more like someone's grandmother than a driver of cars.

"About half an hour," the woman said. "You're lucky the blizzard held off. Another couple of hours and you probably wouldn't have made it in."

"Blizzard?"

"We're expecting ten to fifteen inches by nightfall."

Well, that was good news then. He couldn't very well send her packing if she couldn't go, now could he?

He could be gone himself. And then she could be trapped outside his mountain cottage in her fashion boots for the duration.

But she knew him. He'd be there. All alone. Licking his wounds. Figuring out a way to right wrongs.

Because that was James. And Craig, too, for that matter.

The question was, would he let her help?

Not that she was going to think about that now. No sense in getting herself worked up. No, she'd concentrate instead on the sky. And the clouds. The gift of car heaters.

And writing to James.

That was what she did when life got tough.

OUT IN HIS STUDIO, Craig heard the knocking at the front door. Probably Jenny, coming over to bug him some more. She and her new fiancé were in town for a week and once she'd known Craig was back early from his California Christmas trip, she'd taken it upon herself to watch out for him.

He didn't need to be watched out for. Craig McKellips, just like James Winston Malone before him, watched out for himself.

Which was why he ignored the knocking. And the pounding that followed. Applying colorless color to an abstract airplane with fastidious care.

"James?"

He stopped. Dropped the brush. Rubbed his eyes. He'd been working sixteen hours straight. No wonder he was hearing things.

"James?"

Hearing things twice? That was a new one.

"Okay, I see a light on, I know you're in there." The voice was coming closer. And had a little more trepidation than his imagination usually conjured up.

He stood. Wiped his hands with one of the towels that were always lying around his work space. Went to the door to look out. Just in case.

If no one was out there, no one would see or know. He'd keep his little secret.

"James, I know you're mad at me." The voice was right outside the door. "And I don't blame you. I behaved like a spoiled brat and I have no excuse. Just an explanation. And an apology. If you'll just open the door—"

He pulled it open with force, intending to give the empty space beyond a piece of his mind…loudly. Loud enough to drown out the voices in his head.

"Marybeth?"

"I'm sorry." Appearing slightly ridiculous in a heavy sweater and jeans and thin, soaked boots, she stood there with a duffel over her shoulder.

"For what?" he asked, while he took stock of the situation. Marybeth was there. Outside his studio.

Really.

With wet feet.

"For sending you away. For being a twit. For throwing away the only thing in life I really want. The only thing I've ever wanted. You."

"I lied to you." A blast of cold air hit him—finally. Waking him up a bit.

He'd thought they'd been going to sit down and talk things through on the twenty-sixth after she'd had her time alone and her shower. Instead she'd calmly handed him a refund for his week's rent and asked him to leave. She'd made arrangements to spend a couple of days with the Mathers. Bonnie had been on her way over.

All chances of changing her mind firmly squashed.

"You didn't lie about the things I care about," she said now. "You didn't lie about your heart. Or any of the things you taught me. You didn't lie about the me you saw. Most importantly you didn't lie about seventeen years of faithful friendship."

Her lips were trembling, but it was the tears beading on his beloved's lashes that brought Craig to life.

"You're freezing. Come in," he said, grabbing her hand and pulling her inside. He meant to let her go. To sit down and talk or something. Instead he just kept holding on. And she just kept coming. Until she was pressed tightly against him, her arms clutching him as closely as he was her, and her lips were plastered against his.

Craig kissed her. He was good at that. And wanted to. He held her. He was good with that, too.

But when he felt a prick of moisture at the back of his eyes, he didn't approve. Didn't like it. Didn't accept it.

He wasn't going to cry.

James Winston Malone Craig whatever did not cry. Ever.

"I'm here, my love." The whispered words reached into his darkness, pricking it.

"I'm so sorry I didn't get it right away, that I let you down."

No. She had it wrong. He'd let her down. He'd lived a lie for more than half his life. Forced her to live a lie.

With her arms around his neck, she held his gaze while he struggled to hold his tears.

"I love you, James Winston Malone. And I love you, Craig McKellips. More than that, I am completely, totally, head over heels in love with both of you."

He needed to speak. To support her. To tell her everything was going to be fine. But when he opened his mouth, it trembled. And his vision blurred.

"All your life you've been there for me," she said. "Giving your life to me. And I took and took and took and the minute you showed me you were human, I retreated. I'm so sorry, my love. I will never, ever turn my back on you again. This I promise."

Nah. This wasn't happening. Sobs weren't coming up from within him.

"You are my life, James. My sweet hero. My man. My imperfect human being who, every day since I've known him, has made me happier than I'd ever been or ever will be without him."

Craig dropped to the love seat he'd spent the first part of the night on and she was there. Holding him.

"That's it, love," she said. "Let it out. All those years, all the pain the young man had to deal with on his own. I wish I'd known. I wish you could have told me. I wish I could have helped you, too."

"Ah, sweetie, you did help." With a deep breath he found his voice. "More than you'll ever know. You were the bright light of my days. My reason for getting up. For getting through the day."

"Wouldn't you say, then that we've paid for something neither one of us even did for far too many years?" she asked. "Isn't it time for the hurting to end?"

He grinned through his tears, though his voice was still shaky when he said, "Do you have something in mind?"

"What do you think?"

"I'm going to get a long letter telling me exactly what you think."

"Nope." She wiped away his tears. "You're going to get the words straight from the source," she told him. "I love you. I want to marry you and have your babies and—"

She stopped and Craig's heart caught. "What?"

"Can you do this—" she motioned around the room "—in California? 'Cause it'd be a little hard for me to move the Orange Blossom here."

For the first time since that dinner with his parents long ago, Craig breathed a completely peaceful breath. "California is my home, sweetie. It's about time I got to live there, don't you think?"

"How soon can you leave?"

"How long do we have?"

"We have a houseful of guests starting on the fifth."

"Then that's how soon I can leave."

They were the last coherent words spoken in that artist's studio that afternoon. Later, as the couple drifted to the cabin beyond, only words of love followed them.

And that New Year's Eve, when Marybeth Lawson lifted her glass to James Winston Malone to toast the New Year, his glass clinked against hers.

*Turn the page to read an excerpt from
Tara Taylor Quinn's exciting new novel—
AT CLOSE RANGE,
coming from MIRA Books next month.*

As *Booklist* has said: she "smoothly blends women's fiction with suspense and adds a dash of romance to construct an emotionally intense, compelling story." And according to the review site *All About Romance,* "Quinn writes touching stories about real people that transcend plot type or genre."

When you read *AT CLOSE RANGE,* you'll enter a world of danger and suspense. A world where, despite risk, friendship still matters and love still has a place.

A world no one describes better than Tara Taylor Quinn.

*AT CLOSE RANGE.
Available in December 2008,
wherever books are sold.*

Susan Campbell stuck her head in Hannah's door after lunch on Friday. "You ready, Judge?"

Sitting at her desk, wearing the black silk robe of her calling, Hannah nodded and accepted the compassionate smile on the face of her twenty-six-year-old judicial assistant.

She *wasn't* ready. How could you ever be ready to do something that was going to anger a large, powerful group of thugs—a group known for getting away with unconscionable acts of violence?

Moving with purpose, she left her chambers and looked both ways as she walked into the secure hallway outside her door, then stepped toward the back entrance of the courtroom.

Her job was to administer justice. Kenny Hill might be convicted by a jury of his peers. If that happened, she'd sentence him to prison—and society would be safer.

But he had brothers. Ivory Nation brothers.

"All rise."

Hannah heard Jaime's spiel about the Honorable Hannah Montgomery, but didn't wait for the bailiff to finish. She took her seat with only the briefest glance at the courtroom. Her deputy was there—standing at attention with his eyes firmly on the defendant, who was seated at the table directly in front of her.

Other deputies were there, too, called by the sheriff's

office to oversee this trial. Members of the press lined the back of the room.

"Be seated," Hannah said clearly. Loudly.

She could do her job. She had no doubt of that. She would do it well.

And she'd deal with the ensuing exhaustion, the emotional panic that sometimes resulted from days like today.

"We are back on the record with case number CR2008-000351. The state vs. Kenneth Hill. Before we bring in the jury, we have a matter before the court concerning new evidence received by the state."

The benches in the back of her courtroom were filled to capacity. Whether the victim had as many supporters as the defendant did, Hannah couldn't be sure, but she didn't think so. She suspected the Ivory Nation ranks had been notified overnight. Was she supposed to consider herself warned? Intimidated?

The defendant's parents, sitting stiffly in the front row, didn't seem to know any of the mostly young men surrounding them.

Bobby Donahue, the group's leader, was not present.

Hannah noted every detail of her surroundings as she held the page she'd written the night before.

"The Court has reviewed the Motion to Suppress testimony, which was filed by Robert Keith on behalf of the defendant, Kenny Hill...."

She continued to read, citing case law brought before her during the motion, reminding the defense that it wasn't within the jurisdiction of trial court to find existing laws unconstitutional. She discussed Arizona statute about allowing prejudicial evidence, specifically with regard to cases where evidence pertaining to a previous case was also pertinent to the current one.

In other words, the victim of Kenny Hill's earlier assault would not be appearing as a victim, but as a witness to the possibility that a certain weapon, used in that crime, had caused injuries in this one.

And then, sticking to the plan she'd devised the night before—not to look up from her notes, even once, not to give them anything, any hint that she was human or afraid—she delivered her findings. "The Court has prepared the following ruling," she said, gaining confidence in herself as her voice remained steady. "It is ordered that the Motion to Suppress be denied."

Funny how a room could be filled with negative energy, with savage anger, that emitted not a sound.

The only thing Hannah could hear was the rapid tapping of her court recorder, fifty-year-old Tammy Rhodes. Jaime, the other person in Hannah's peripheral vision, was staring down at her desk.

"The state is warned that any mention of a previous conviction for this defendant will result in a mistrial."

That was it. She'd reached the end of her ruling. Of her notes. There was nothing to do but look up.

The trial that had already run two days over its time allotment was continued until Monday—the earliest the state's newly approved witness could be brought in. Which meant that the weight hanging over Hannah would be there all weekend.

She and William, a friend and fellow judge, had tickets to a concert at Symphony Hall the next night. His son, a student at a private high school for the arts, was a guest violinist in one piece and as William rarely saw the boy, he'd been thrilled to get the invitation. Hannah hoped, as she drove home on Friday, that she'd be able to stay awake. Put her in a comfortable seat, in a dark room with soft music and…

What was that? She saw a pile in the road by her driveway.

Driving slowly, Hannah tried to identify the curious shape. Her heart was pounding, but she told herself there was no reason for that.

Some trash had fallen from a dispenser during that morning's pickup, that was all.

But the tan and beige with that streak of black. What had she put in her trash? Some kind of packaging, maybe.

What had she purchased? Opened? Had she even bought anything new?

As she drew closer, her pulse quickened again. The blob didn't look like packaging. It looked…furry. Like an animal.

The exact size of Callie Bodacious.

Hannah's beloved eleven-year-old cat. The direct offspring of a gift from the man she'd married—the man who, at seventeen, had been diagnosed with leukemia and, at twenty-three, had died in the bed she'd shared with him.

"No!" Throwing the car in Park in the middle of her quiet street, Hannah got out, the door of the Lexus wide-open behind her as she sped over to the shape in the road.

Callie wasn't a purebred. Wasn't worth much in a monetary sense. She was basically an alley cat. One who wasn't particularly fond of people, other than Hannah.

And she was all the family Hannah had left.

Dropping down on her knees, reaching out to the animal, Hannah blinked back tears so she could see clearly. The black between the eyes told her it was definitely Callie.

And she was still breathing. Sobbing now, Hannah glanced up, around, looking for help. And then grabbed the cell phone out of the case hooked to her waistband.

Addled, frustrated that there was no ambulance she could call for cats, no feline 911, scared out of her wits, she did the next best thing.

He answered. Thank God.

"Brian? Where are you?"

"On my way home. What's wrong?"

"It's Callie! She's hurt. Oh God, Brian, what am I going to do? She needs help and I'm afraid to move her. Her head's at a bad angle."

"What happened?"

"I don't know," Hannah wailed, growing more panicked with every second that passed. "She's in the road so she must've been hit by a car, but I don't see a lot of blood."

Brian asked her to check a couple of things, including lifting the cat's eyelids. And then he told her to sit tight and wait for him.

Brian wished he could say he'd never seen Hannah Montgomery in such a state. Wished it so hard the tension made his head throb. Watching his good friend grieve was not a new thing to him.

And not a distant memory, either. It had been less than a year since he'd sat on this very same sofa, in this very same house, sick at heart, holding this vibrant, beautiful, intelligent woman while she sobbed uncontrollably.

Less than a year since another little body was carried out of this home.

"I...I...she...I...she must've slipped out this morning. And..."

She couldn't finish as another bout of sobs overcame her, the sound harsh, discordant, in the peaceful room.

"I was just...so...pre...pre...preoccupied..."

He held her, resting his chin lightly on her head. He wanted to let her know that he was there. She wasn't alone.

"...the trial..."

His mind froze, attention completely focused as suspicion formed.

"You said you were sure you saw her on her cat tree when you left."

"I…must've…been mistaken…"

Or not.

Looking around the room, all senses on alert, Brian wondered if Hannah's windows and doors were secure. He wondered if they should be calling the police.

Or if he was overreacting.

Surely anyone who meant to do Hannah harm would have done so while she was driving home. Running her off the road. Making it look like an accident.

Instead they'd done…this.

But they wouldn't be so bold as to attack a judge in her own home. That would make them too easy to find. Detectives would know who to question and fingerprint and…

"We need to call the police."

* * * * *

Here is a sneak preview of
A STONE CREEK CHRISTMAS,
the latest in Linda Lael Miller's acclaimed
MℂKETTRICK *series.*

A lonely horse brought vet Olivia O'Ballivan to Tanner
Quinn's farm, but it's the rancher's love that might cause
her to stay.

A STONE CREEK CHRISTMAS
Available December 2008
from Silhouette Special Edition

Tanner heard the rig roll in around sunset. Smiling, he wandered to the window. Watched as Olivia O'Ballivan climbed out of her Suburban, flung one defiant glance toward the house and started for the barn, the golden retriever trotting along behind her.

Taking his coat and hat down from the peg next to the back door, he put them on and went outside. He was used to being alone, even liked it, but keeping company with Doc O'Ballivan, bristly though she sometimes was, would provide a welcome diversion.

He gave her time to reach the horse Butterpie's stall, then walked into the barn.

The golden retriever came to greet him, all wagging tail and melting brown eyes, and he bent to stroke her soft, sturdy back. "Hey, there, dog," he said.

Sure enough, Olivia was in the stall, brushing Butterpie down and talking to her in a soft, soothing voice that touched something private inside Tanner and made him want to turn on one heel and beat it back to the house.

He'd be damned if he'd do it, though.

This was *his* ranch, *his* barn. Well-intentioned as she was, *Olivia* was the trespasser here, not him.

"She's still very upset," Olivia told him, without turning to look at him or slowing down with the brush.

Shiloh, always an easy horse to get along with, stood contentedly in his own stall, munching away on the feed Tanner had given him earlier. Butterpie, he noted, hadn't touched her supper as far as he could tell.

"Do you know anything at all about horses, Mr. Quinn?" Olivia asked.

He leaned against the stall door, the way he had the day before, and grinned. He'd practically been raised on horseback; he and Tessa had grown up on their grandmother's farm in the Texas hill country, after their folks divorced and went their separate ways, both of them too busy to bother with a couple of kids. "A few things," he said. "And I mean to call you Olivia, so you might as well return the favor and address me by my first name."

He watched as she took that in, dealt with it, decided on an approach. He'd have to wait and see what that turned out to be, but he didn't mind. It was a pleasure just watching Olivia O'Ballivan grooming a horse.

"All right, *Tanner,*" she said. "This barn is a disgrace. When are you going to have the roof fixed? If it snows again, the hay will get wet and probably mold…"

He chuckled, shifted a little. He'd have a crew out there the following Monday morning to replace the roof and shore up the walls—he'd made the arrangements over a week before—but he felt no particular compunction to explain that. He was enjoying her ire too much; it made her color rise and her hair fly when she turned her head, and the faster breathing made her perfect breasts go up and down in an enticing rhythm.

"What makes you so sure I'm a greenhorn?" he asked mildly, still leaning on the gate.

At last she looked straight at him, but she didn't move from Butterpie's side. "Your hat, your boots—that fancy red truck you drive. I'll bet it's customized."

Tanner grinned. Adjusted his hat. "Are you telling me real cowboys don't drive red trucks?"

"There are lots of trucks around here," she said. "Some of them are red, and some of them are new. And *all* of them are splattered with mud or manure or both."

"Maybe I ought to put in a car wash, then," he teased. "Sounds like there's a market for one. Might be a good investment."

She softened, though not significantly, and spared him a cautious half smile, full of questions she probably wouldn't ask. "There's a good car wash in Indian Rock," she informed him. "People go there. It's only forty miles."

"Oh," he said with just a hint of mockery. "*Only* forty miles. Well, then. Guess I'd better dirty up my truck if I want to be taken seriously in these here parts. Scuff up my boots a bit, too, and maybe stomp on my hat a couple of times."

Her cheeks went a fetching shade of pink. "You are twisting what I said," she told him, brushing Butterpie again, her touch gentle but sure. "I meant…"

Tanner envied that little horse. Wished he had a furry hide, so he'd need brushing, too.

"You *meant* that I'm not a real cowboy," he said. "And you could be right. I've spent a lot of time on construction sites over the last few years, or in meetings where a hat and boots wouldn't be appropriate. Instead of digging out my old gear, once I decided to take this job, I just bought new."

"I bet you don't even *have* any old gear," she challenged, but she was smiling, albeit cautiously, as though she might withdraw into a disapproving frown at any second.

He took off his hat, extended it to her. "Here," he teased. "Rub that around in the muck until it suits you."

She laughed, and the sound—well, it caused a powerful and wholly unexpected shift inside him. Scared the hell out of him and, paradoxically, made him yearn to hear it again.

* * * * *

Discover how this rugged rancher's wanderlust is tamed in time for a merry Christmas, in
A STONE CREEK CHRISTMAS.
In stores December 2008.

Silhouette®

SPECIAL EDITION™

FROM *NEW YORK TIMES* BESTSELLING AUTHOR

LINDA LAEL MILLER

A STONE CREEK CHRISTMAS

Veterinarian Olivia O'Ballivan finds the animals in Stone Creek playing Cupid between her and Tanner Quinn. Even Tanner's daughter, Sophie, is eager to play matchmaker. With everyone conspiring against them and the holiday season fast approaching, Tanner and Olivia may just get everything they want for Christmas after all!

Available December 2008
wherever books are sold.

HARLEQUIN® *Romance*®

Marry-Me Christmas

by *USA TODAY* bestselling author

SHIRLEY JUMP

A *Bride* FOR ALL *Seasons*

Ruthless and successful journalist Flynn never mixes business with pleasure. But when he's sent to write a scathing review of Samantha's bakery, her beauty and innocence catches him off guard. Has this small-town girl unlocked the city slicker's heart?

Available December 2008.

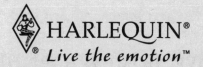

HARLEQUIN®
Live the emotion™

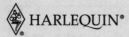

HARLEQUIN®

American ★ Romance®

HOLLY JACOBS
Once Upon a Christmas

Daniel McLean is thrilled to learn he
may be the father of Michelle Hamilton's
nephew. When Daniel starts to spend
time with Brandon and help her organize
Erie Elementary's big Christmas Fair, the
three discover a paternity test won't make
them a family, but the love they discover
just might....

Available December 2008
wherever books are sold.

LOVE, HOME & HAPPINESS

Harlequin® Historical
Historical Romantic Adventure!

THE MISTLETOE WAGER
Christine Merrill

Harry Pennyngton, Earl of Anneslea,
is surprised when his estranged wife,
Helena, arrives home for Christmas.
Especially when she's intent on
divorce! A festive house party
is in full swing when the guests
are snowed in, and Harry and
Helena find they are together
under the mistletoe....

*Available December 2008
wherever books are sold.*

REQUEST YOUR FREE BOOKS!

2 FREE NOVELS PLUS 2 FREE GIFTS!

HARLEQUIN®

Super Romance®

Exciting, emotional, unexpected!

YES! Please send me 2 FREE Harlequin Superromance® novels and my 2 FREE gifts (gifts are worth about $10). After receiving them, if I don't wish to receive any more books, I can return the shipping statement marked "cancel." If I don't cancel, I will receive 6 brand-new novels every month and be billed just $4.69 per book in the U.S. or $5.24 per book in Canada, plus 25¢ shipping and handling per book and applicable taxes, if any*. That's a savings of close to 15% off the cover price! I understand that accepting the 2 free books and gifts places me under no obligation to buy anything. I can always return a shipment and cancel at any time. Even if I never buy another book from Harlequin, the two free books and gifts are mine to keep forever.

135 HDN EEX7   336 HDN EEYK

Name	(PLEASE PRINT)	
Address		Apt. #
City	State/Prov.	Zip/Postal Code

Signature (if under 18, a parent or guardian must sign)

Mail to the **Harlequin Reader Service:**
IN U.S.A.: P.O. Box 1867, Buffalo, NY 14240-1867
IN CANADA: P.O. Box 609, Fort Erie, Ontario L2A 5X3

Not valid to current subscribers of Harlequin Superromance books.

Want to try two free books from another line?
Call 1-800-873-8635 or visit www.morefreebooks.com.

* Terms and prices subject to change without notice. N.Y. residents add applicable sales tax. Canadian residents will be charged applicable provincial taxes and GST. Offer not valid in Quebec. This offer is limited to one order per household. All orders subject to approval. Credit or debit balances in a customer's account(s) may be offset by any other outstanding balance owed by or to the customer. Please allow 4 to 6 weeks for delivery. Offer available while quantities last.

Your Privacy: Harlequin is committed to protecting your privacy. Our Privacy Policy is available online at www.eHarlequin.com or upon request from the Reader Service. From time to time we make our lists of customers available to reputable third parties who may have a product or service of interest to you. If you would prefer we not share your name and address, please check here. ☐

HSR08R

Inside ROMANCE

Stay up-to-date on all your romance reading news!

The Inside Romance newsletter is a FREE quarterly newsletter highlighting our upcoming series releases and promotions!

Click on the <u>Inside Romance</u> link on the front page of **www.eHarlequin.com** or e-mail us at insideromance@harlequin.ca to sign up to receive your FREE newsletter today!

You can also subscribe by writing us at: HARLEQUIN BOOKS Attention: Customer Service Department P.O. Box 9057, Buffalo, NY 14269-9057

Please allow 4-6 weeks for delivery of the first issue by mail.

HARLEQUIN
Super Romance

COMING NEXT MONTH

#1530 A MAN TO RELY ON • Cindi Myers
Going Back

Scandal seems to follow Marisol Luna. And this trip home is no exception. She's not staying long in this town that can't forget who she was. Then she falls for Scott Redmond. Suddenly he's making her forget the gossip and rethink her exit plan.

#1531 NO PLACE LIKE HOME • Margaret Watson
The McInnes Triplets

All Bree McInnes has to do is make it through the summer without anyone discovering her secrets. But keeping a low profile turns out to be harder than the single mom thought—especially when her sexy professor-boss begins to fall in love. With her!

#1532 HIS ONLY DEFENSE • Carolyn McSparren
Count on a Cop

Cop rule number one: don't fall in love with a perp. Too bad Liz Gibson forgot that one. Except unlike everybody else, she doesn't believe Jud Slaughter killed his wife. Now she has to prove his innocence or lose him forever.

#1533 FOR THE SAKE OF THE CHILDREN • Cynthia Reese
You, Me & the Kids

Dana Wilson is *exactly* what Lissa thinks her single father needs. Dana is a single mom *and* the new school nurse. Lissa's dad, Patrick Connor, is chair of the board of education! Perfect? Well, there may be a few wrinkles that need ironing out....

#1534 THE SON BETWEEN THEM • Molly O'Keefe
A Little Secret

Samantha Riggins keeps pulling J. D. Kronos back. With her he is a better man and can forget his P.I. world. But when he discovers the secret she's been hiding, nothing is the same. And now J.D. must choose between his former life and a new one with Samantha.

#1535 MEANT FOR EACH OTHER • Lee Duran
Everlasting Love

Since the moment they met, Frankie has loved Johnny Davis. Yet their love hasn't always been enough to make things work. Then Johnny is injured and needs her. As she rushes to his side, Frankie discovers the true value of being meant for each other.